"You need to at ~~...~~
like me in public ~~...~~
daughter's sake. ~~...~~

Like a splash of cold ~~...~~
days were truly gone. Cole had zero interest ~~...~~
her except as Mary Kate's mother.

"We have a child together," he said. "I don't
want us to be enemies."

"Given our past, I don't see how we can be
friends," she said stiffly. "Our relationship has
to be strictly business."

His jaw tightened. "Business it is."

Even though she was pushing him away as
hard as she could, deep inside a tiny piece of
Jane's heart chipped.

Which was odd, because she hadn't thought
there was anything left to break.

Dear Reader,

Teenage pregnancy seems to keep cropping up in my books in one form or another. I think that's because the conflict is inbuilt. Having a baby can be the most joyous experience in a woman's life, but if you're young, without money, a job or a life partner, you're bound to have a few worries. If you're ambitious like Jane, the heroine in *How To Trap a Parent*, you have to work out your priorities early on.

We hardly ever consider the boy's role or feelings. My hero, Cole, fathered not one but *two* babies to different girls when he was a teenager. Talk about anxiety! He married one girl out of duty, lost the one he loved and missed out on a daughter's early years.

This book is about a lot of things – family, home, vineyards, horses, daughters and sisters, thwarted ambitions and dreams fulfilled. But mostly it's about a love affair that blossoms again after years apart.

I hope you enjoy Jane and Cole's story as much as I enjoyed writing it. I love to hear from readers. You can e-mail me at www.joankilby. com or write to me at PO Box 234, Point Roberts, WA 98281-0234, Australia.

Joan Kilby

How To Trap
a Parent

JOAN KILBY

MILLS & BOON®
Pure reading pleasure™

First published in Great Britain 2009
by Harlequin Mills & Boon Limited,
Eton House, 18-24 Paradise Road, Richmond, Surrey TW9 1SR

ISBN: 978 0 263 87375 7

38-0609

Harlequin Mills & Boon policy is to use papers that are
natural, renewable and recyclable products and made from
wood grown in sustainable forests. The logging and
manufacturing processes conform to the legal environmental
regulations of the country of origin.

Printed and bound in Spain
by Litografía Rosés S.A., Barcelona

ABOUT THE AUTHOR

When Joan Kilby isn't working on her next romance novel, she can often be found sipping a latte at a pavement café and indulging in her favorite pastime of people watching. Originally from Vancouver, Canada, she now lives in Australia with her husband and three children. She enjoys cooking as a creative outlet and gets some of her best story ideas while watching her Jack Russell terrier chase waves at the beach.

CHAPTER ONE

JANE LINDEN PARKED her black Mazda in front of Red Hill Real Estate and checked her hair in the visor mirror. Just her luck! The only person in this small rural town who could sell her late aunt's farm for her was Cole Roberts, the man who'd broken her heart thirteen years ago. Cole wasn't a *bad* man; in fact, she'd never known anyone as loyal to his family. But that didn't mean he hadn't made her suffer.

Hitching her red leather tote higher on her shoulder, Jane climbed out of the car. Seeing him again would *not* be a problem. She was *over* him; him and his green eyes and killer grin. She'd be in and out of Red Hill faster than she could snap her fingers. And he would never know she'd cried herself to sleep for three years because he'd married Leslie Stanwyck instead of her.

All that had happened a long time ago. Jane was a different person, older and wiser. She might not have made a name for herself in Hollywood, but those acting lessons Rafe had given her way back when were finally going to pay off. Bright and breezy, that's the way she'd play it. Ignore the pain, hide the anger; Cole no longer meant a thing to her. How could he? Thirteen years was way too long to carry a torch.

A bell tinkled as she entered through the glass door of the real estate agency. A small seating area was to her right, reception to her left. The young woman behind the curved desk wore black rectangular glasses and had fine dark hair swept into a ponytail.

Leslie's little sister. The last time Jane had seen this girl she'd worn pigtails and Bratz T-shirts. Jane pushed her sunglasses up into her hair. "Millie?"

Millie glanced up with a bright smile. "Hi, um… Do I know you?"

"Jane Linden. I went to high school

with Leslie." She glanced past reception to the narrow hall and the private offices. "Is Cole in?"

"I'll see if he's available." Millie reached for the phone.

"He and I are old friends. I'll surprise him." Jane hurried past before Millie could stop her. Old friends, indeed. They'd been far more to each other than friends; and in the end, far less.

Through the glass wall of his office she could see Cole working on something at his desk, his brow creased in concentration as he chewed on the end of a pencil. In spite of her pep talk, her heart turned over at the sight of his face, still familiar even though she hadn't seen him in three years, the time he'd come to L.A. to visit Mary Kate.

Steeling herself, she knocked once and opened the door. "Well, just look at you! All dressed up in a suit and tie behind a big fancy desk. You're quite the successful businessman."

Cole started at her voice, his eyebrows lifting as he set aside his pencil and newspaper. He smoothed a hand lightly over his neatly combed dark brown hair. "Jane! I'm surprised to see you back in Red Hill so soon." He glanced past her eagerly. "Did you bring Mary Kate this time?"

Jane had come alone four weeks earlier to arrange her aunt Esther's funeral. Mary Kate had stayed in L.A. with friends. She'd had the lead in the classroom concert as well as end-of-term exams.

"She's at the farmhouse." Jane's grip on her tote strap tightened. As the girl's father, Cole had rights whether she liked it or not. *Bright and breezy,* she reminded herself and pasted on a smile. "We arrived yesterday. We're both still jet-lagged so I let Mary Kate stay home."

"Have a seat," Cole said. "I'm sorry about your aunt Esther. She was so young."

"Thanks." Jane sat stiffly on the edge of the visitor's chair. "Her heart attack was unexpected."

"I'm sorry I missed the funeral," Cole continued formally. "I was closing a deal on a house that afternoon or I would've come. I called you the next day but you must have already left."

"I was only in town a few days," Jane explained, shifting in her chair. It was hard to be bright when the subject was so sad, hard to be breezy when the conversation was this stilted. "I had work commitments and wanted to be back for Christmas."

"How long are you in Australia?"

Jane forced herself to relax and sink back into the chair. Her short white skirt slid halfway up her thigh. She saw his gaze drop before he quickly glanced away. She tugged the fabric down. "We're back for good. Goodbye, L.A., hello, Melbourne. I've got a job as a publicist with Moonray Productions. In fact, I've hit the ground running, publicizing the premiere of a movie called *Swept Away.*"

"You mean it?" he said. "You're back?"

She nodded. "A moving company is packing up my house in Pasadena and shipping everything down here."

"That's wonderful news," Cole said, smiling for the first time. "I'll be able to get to know Mary Kate properly. Stephanie will be excited."

"How is Stephanie?" Jane asked politely. "Does she live with you?"

"She's great. She stays with me on the weekends and during the summer holidays and with Leslie during the week when school's in." He angled a framed photo on his desk so Jane could see the picture of a young girl with Cole's open grin and Leslie's straight blond hair. "She's turning twelve next month. Loves horses."

"Mary Kate, too," Jane said, softening.

"Yeah?" Cole's face lit.

Something like warmth flashed between them, a shared moment over their daughter. Then Cole leaned back in his chair, his face carefully neutral.

"Leslie's married to Fergus Palmer now," Cole went on. "They have two little boys from his first marriage."

"So I heard." Cole's divorce from Leslie had gone through before his trip to L.A. At first Jane had wondered if he'd been hoping to get back together with her, but his interest had proved to be solely in Mary Kate.

Cole glanced at her bare left hand. "What about you? Are you still seeing that producer you introduced me to in L.A.?"

"That was a long time ago. Anyway, I don't have time for a relationship," Jane said. "Mary Kate and I are a self-contained unit. We don't need anyone else."

Cole came upright with a thump of his chair legs on the mat. "You can't decide that for Mary Kate. She has family here. Me, Stephanie, her grandmother and her uncle Joey—"

Jane held up a hand, shifting back to the edge of her seat. Any hint of warmth had vanished and the time for polite chitchat was definitely over. "She'll see you all, don't worry."

They glared at each other, unmoving.

Then Cole let out a breath and flexed his shoulders. Unexpectedly, he gave her the grin that used to twist her heart into knots. "Doesn't take much to set us off, does it?"

Jane smiled stiffly, keeping a tight grip on herself, refusing to respond to that grin. So much for bright and breezy.

Cole cleared his throat and changed the

subject. "Have you come home to live at Cockatoo Ridge?"

"No," Jane said. "That's why I'm here. Esther's will has gone through probate and her estate has been settled. I want you to sell Cockatoo Ridge for me."

"You're selling the farm?"

She supposed she could hardly blame him if his surprise was mingled with a touch of resentment—if not outrage. She could hardly blame him if it was. Cockatoo Ridge had been built by his great-grandfather and had belonged to his family for generations until Cole's father had been forced to sell it to pay gambling debts. No doubt Cole would love to have it back, but she couldn't afford to be sentimental. Cole was unlikely to be able to meet the high price the property would rightfully command.

"I have no use for the land," she explained. "The house is old and needs work. I've got my eye on a high-rise apartment in the city. It's right on the waterfront, a corner apartment with fabulous views of the bay. There are theaters and restaurants nearby and it's close to work."

"Sounds expensive."

"It costs a bomb. That's why I need to sell the farm straightaway. For the highest possible price."

"Those are mutually exclusive criteria," Cole informed her, suddenly businesslike. "You can sell quickly for a lower price or wait for a decent offer. Midsummer isn't the best time to sell. Why not enjoy the warm months in Red Hill and put the property on the market in autumn?"

And give her horse-crazy daughter a chance to settle into a country home and not want to leave? No way. "If I wait, I could lose the apartment."

Cole tapped his pen on the blotter, frowning at her in silence. Then, with a sigh, he pulled out his appointment book and turned the pages. "I'll come out and value the farm and we can settle on an asking price."

"It hasn't changed since your family lived there—a rambling Victorian house and barn on ten acres with a creek running through it. Do you really need to see it?" The less she saw of *him,* the better.

"It's been years since I was at Cockatoo Ridge," Cole said. "I wouldn't be doing my job if I didn't inspect the property in person."

Jane nodded, resigning herself. "How about tomorrow? I'm heading back to Melbourne on Sunday night."

"You always were in a desperate hurry to leave town."

She eyed him steadily. "I still am."

"I wish I could get you to reconsider," he said, his gaze hardening. "This is an opportunity for me to get to know Mary Kate. I've had precious little contact with her over the years."

Jane took a deep breath and counted to ten. Mary Kate talked to Cole on the phone on birthdays and at Christmas. She replied to his e-mails. Was it Jane's fault the time difference made communication difficult? Or that an almost-twelve-year-old had little interest in a faraway father she'd never known and rarely saw?

"It's not easy finding the time and money to make overseas trips," she said. "I came back when she was five. You've been over a couple of times."

"The last time I was only in L.A. for a week before you whisked her off to Canada on a trip you'd neglected to mention before I flew all the way over there."

Jane jiggled a sandal-clad foot impatiently. "It was a last-minute thing. She'd been invited to the Calgary Stampede by a classmate and begged me to let her go."

"There were other times I asked to visit, but there was always some reason it wasn't convenient."

"And there were times when I suggested you come and you had other plans," Jane reminded him. "It's not that I don't want you to see her—" She broke off abruptly, unable to speak her real fears aloud—that Cole would try to take Mary Kate away from her.

"I hope not. She's *my* daughter, too." Cole's voice took on an edge, sounding to Jane almost like a threat.

Her chin rose. "I bore her, I gave birth to her, I raised her. She's *mine*. You have Stephanie. Isn't that enough?"

"If I had *ten* children, I would still want Mary Kate," Cole insisted. "Kids aren't stuffed toys. When you've got enough you don't mind giving one away. I wish you'd never left Red Hill with my child."

"Did you really imagine Mary Kate and I could have lived in this small town and played second fiddle to Leslie and Stephanie?" Jane demanded. She'd known he'd been going out with Leslie but the couple had broken up before Leslie had gone on holiday with her parents. Then Leslie had come home pregnant. Cole's future had been stitched up within a week, long before Jane had had any inkling that *she* was also pregnant.

Cole was silent, his jaw tightening. Throwing her an unreadable glance, he pulled out an appointment card and began to write on it.

Jane tilted her head, studying him. Who wore ties nowadays or combed their hair with a part? He was like Clark Kent, the handsome nerd who doesn't make the most of his sex appeal. "You haven't changed."

"You're wrong," he said flatly. "As you frequently are, but there's no telling *you* that."

He rose and came around the desk. Jane

got to her feet, trapped between Cole and the wall. He held out the card. She tried to take it but he wouldn't let it go.

"Well?" he asked. "Am I going to see Mary Kate?"

"Of course you're going to see Mary Kate," she said, tugging at the card. "Are you going to help me out, or should I go hire an agent in Dromana?"

Cole released the card. "Ten o'clock tomorrow morning."

Jane spun on her heel and strode to the door, her red tote bumping against her hip, her hands shaking. She breezed past Millie, throwing her the brightest smile she could manage. All she could think of now was getting to her car.

COLE LET OUT a deep breath and tugged on his collar as Jane hurried away. It felt two sizes too small, as if he'd somehow swelled with frustration at having to deal with Jane. She was as elusive as ever, slipping out of his grasp before he could close his fist. He'd thought he'd cared for her once, but now she was just an obstacle to his being with his daughter.

"You haven't changed either," he said softly, moving to the corridor to watch through the window of the outer office as she crossed the road. "Still have to have the upper hand."

He'd been unbelievably careless, getting both Leslie and Jane pregnant back when he was eighteen. He and they had been paying the price for it ever since. A failed marriage, a single mum raising a daughter he barely knew. The opportunity had now arisen for him to rectify at least one of those wrongs. He didn't know why Jane was so possessive of Mary Kate but he *would* spend time with the girl, whether Jane liked it or not.

His younger brother, Joey, came out of his office across the hall, munching on an apple. He was tieless and his shirtsleeves were rolled up. A lock of near-black hair hung over his forehead. "Was that Jane Linden? Has she got the kid with her?"

Cole nodded. "At the farm."

"I forget, who's older, Mary Kate or Stephanie?"

"They're both nearly twelve. Mary Kate's six weeks younger than Stephanie." Cole couldn't believe how quickly the girls were growing up. As annoying as Jane was, he was pleased she was back in the country. It was time he asserted his rights as a father.

Joey lounged in Cole's doorway, still gnawing on his apple. "You gonna see her?"

"Mary Kate? Of course I'm going to see her. As much and as often as Jane'll let me."

"No, I mean Jane. As in *see* her."

Cole stared at his brother. "Why on earth would I want to do that?"

"You used to be in love with her," Joey stated matter-of-factly. "Maybe you'll get back together."

"I doubt it. She's only in town to sell Cockatoo Ridge."

Joey took a huge bite and gestured with the core. "*You* should buy it."

"Using what for money?" Cole said bitterly. He should have inherited the farm and be living there now. Checking his watch, he added, "Aren't you supposed to at the Terpstra open house in five minutes?"

"Yeah, yeah, I'm going. Nobody ever shows up to these things on time." Joey tossed his apple core into the rubbish bin and pushed himself off the door frame.

"Actually, they do. As the agent, you're expected to take care of certain things beforehand." Jeez, he'd gone over this repeatedly. "Speak to the vendors, set out the signs—"

"Dude, if you weren't cranking away at me, I'd be there by now." Joey sauntered toward the exit that led to the employees' car park. He paused on the threshold and some of the cockiness went out of his face. "Listen, Cole, I need a favor."

"Sure, what is it?"

"I need to borrow some money."

"How much?" Cole asked, reaching for his wallet.

"Two hundred dollars. Three would be better." Joey picked a piece of apple skin out of his teeth with his fingernail.

"Three hundred dollars." Frowning, Cole made no move to take out the money. "You just got paid last week."

"I know but… Crystal and I went to the

casino last night and well, we dropped a wad at the blackjack table."

"Joey!" Cole began then lowered his voice, mindful of Millie in the outer office. "Remember what happened to Dad? You don't want to go down the same path."

"It's not like I'm addicted," Joey said. "We had a bit of a flutter. Small potatoes."

"You'll just have to tighten your belt until the next paycheck," Cole replied.

"I've got bills due," Joey argued. "They eat up most of my wages. Not that I don't appreciate you giving me a job, but if I was allowed to show the more expensive listings I'd make better commissions."

"You've only been qualified as an agent for six months," Cole reminded him. "You've got to earn the right, learn the ropes, before you get access to the top houses."

"Come on, dude. It's just a loan. If I don't make a car payment soon I'll lose my wheels," Joey added. "Then how will I pay you back?"

This argument always landed Cole in a catch-22 situation and Joey knew it. His little brother was nearly twenty-two but in many ways still a child. At his age Cole had been married with a young daughter and supporting his mother and Joey as well. Would his brother *ever* grow up and take responsibility for himself?

"Here." He handed over a cluster of fifty-dollar bills. "But I won't be forking out money every time you lose at the casino."

"Thanks, mate." Joey gave Cole the thumbs-up. "You're the best. I'll call Crystal and tell her not to pawn her grandmother's wedding ring." Joey whipped out his cell phone as he strode toward the exit door.

Cole went back to his office and shut the door. He closed his eyes, took slow deep breaths and willed his blood pressure to drop. He fell into a familiar daydream, visualizing himself walking between rows of grapevines, running a hand over the fluttering leaves, admiring the thick twisting stems and the clusters of ripe grapes. Clods of red dirt crunched beneath his boots.

He'd had his eye on Cockatoo Ridge for years, saving everything he could while he watched helplessly as land prices rose steadily, keeping the farm always just out of reach. Now the property was for sale…

What was he thinking? He still wasn't ready.

JANE LIFTED a beautiful jade-green vase with a delicate black design made by her aunt off the mantelpiece and put it in a safe spot in the china cabinet. Then she swept knickknacks off the marble surface into an empty cardboard box. It was hard clearing out her aunt's things but keeping busy helped her cope with her grief. Besides, there was no one else to do it.

Jane, an only child, had lived with her parents in Sydney until they'd both died in a scuba diving accident when she was eight. Esther had raised her after that, first in a tiny terrace house in inner Melbourne, then at Cockatoo Ridge Farm where they'd moved when Jane started high school, so Esther could have her own pottery studio. Since Jane's abrupt departure from Red Hill thirteen years ago, she'd seen Esther mainly in L.A. where her aunt had connections with gallery owners. In the interim, her aunt had gradually filled the farmhouse with furniture, dishes and ornaments from secondhand stores.

Jane carried the box out to the garage where she was collecting things to be disposed of. Back in the living room, she gazed in dismay at the remaining clutter and groaned.

"What's the matter, Mom?" Mary Kate came into the room eating a piece of toast smeared with jam. With her beads and bangles, bare midriff and miniskirt, she looked more like fifteen than eleven-going-on-twelve.

"Nothing that a few gallons of petrol and a lit match wouldn't fix," Jane muttered.

"I heard you groan," Mary Kate insisted. "I wouldn't be surprised if you got sick here. The water tastes funny."

"It's bore water," Jane told her. "Perfectly good. In fact it's purer than town water. What you're tasting is an absence of chemicals."

Mary Kate brushed invisible dirt off the

seat of an ancient green brocade armchair and perched on the edge. She held her elbows in close to her sides so they wouldn't touch the stained fabric and nibbled her toast. "How could Aunt Esther live like this?"

Jane picked up a framed photo of her aunt at her potter's wheel. Esther's dark hair was streaked lightly with gray and pulled back in a long ponytail. Her jeans and plaid shirt were spattered, her thin face set in concentration as her long fingers shaped the spinning cylinder of clay. "She focused more on her work than on house-keeping, that's for sure. But she was an important potter. One of her pieces is in the National Gallery."

"I just don't get why she collected so much stuff."

"Tell me about it," Jane sighed. "I hardly know where to start." She glanced at her watch. "Are you almost finished? Your father will arrive any minute."

"I'm still eating. I just put an egg on to boil."

"That's okay. I'm sure he won't mind."

Mary Kate bit her lip. "Do I *have* to see him?"

"I thought you wanted to." Jane pushed her daughter's fringe back to peer into Mary Kate's eyes. "Are you feeling okay?"

"I'm fine." Mary Kate turned her face away. "But I—"

The cell phone clipped to Jane's hip pocket chimed, and she reached for it. "Excuse me, honey.

"Otto." He was a Melbourne journalist she'd contacted to publicize the premiere. Jane went into her aunt's study and sat at the rolltop desk where she'd temporarily set up her office. "I'm scheduling interviews with the leads of *Swept Away*—Rafe Baldwyn and Mia MacDonald. Let me find my diary and I'll tell you what times are available."

A doorbell sounded.

"Otto, I'll call you back." Jane hurried out to open the door and passed through the lounge room in time to see Mary Kate hurrying toward the kitchen. "Hey, where are you going? He's not going to bite you. Come back here."

"In a minute." Mary Kate ducked through the door.

What was wrong with that girl? Jane walked the dark red carpet runner covering the scratched floorboards of the hall. She brushed back her hair, smoothed down her skirt and opened the door. Cole stood on the veranda, a folded clipboard in hand. His dark hair was perfectly styled, his light brown suit immaculate, his expression politely neutral. He appeared so smooth and composed that Jane couldn't contain the impulse to ruffle his feathers.

"You look like a real estate agent from central casting." She jammed her hands on her hips and eyed him up and down. "If I was a director, I'd be looking for the flaw that shows you're human."

"If I have flaws, I take care to hide them," Cole said evenly.

"Isn't that just like a man?" *And what a man.* Squashing that thought, Jane said, "Come in."

CHAPTER TWO

COLE FOLLOWED Jane down the hall to the lounge room. He could almost smell his mother's Sunday roast cooking and hear his dog Toby's tail thump in greeting.

His family had kept chickens, a few sheep and a couple of horses. His father had worked at the real estate agency; his mother had stayed home and looked after the animals and the vegetable garden. He and Joey had roamed freely for miles around through woods and fields on horseback. With the nostalgia came an acute sense of loss, for those long-ago days and for what he might have done with the farm as an adult.

"You can hardly see the house for the contents, but I'm gradually clearing it out," Jane said.

On closer inspection Cole observed the dingy paintwork and chipped plaster. On the high ceiling a water stain ran from one corner to the pressed-tin rose in the center. It made him sad and angry to see the house his great-grandfather had built in such poor condition. Keeping his expression impassive, he made a note on his clipboard.

"Esther allowed the house to get rundown." Jane seemed to know what he was thinking.

"It just needs a little TLC," Cole said, running a hand along the polished marble mantelpiece covered in patches of dust. "You haven't changed your mind about selling? You might like Red Hill. It's more sophisticated than it was in the old days."

"My work is in the city," Jane said. "And Mary Kate is looking forward to starting high school there next month and making new friends."

Cole glanced toward the kitchen where he could smell toast. "Where is Mary Kate?"

"She went to check on her egg. She's still having breakfast." Jane led the way into the large country kitchen filled with half-packed boxes of Esther's dishes. The back door was open and Mary Kate was gone. "I guess she stepped out for a minute. I suggested earlier that she take a walk down to the creek. She probably decided to do it before you rang the doorbell."

"Of course." Cole studied Jane's averted face. Why did he have the feeling she was hiding something? Why would Mary Kate go out and leave a pot bubbling away on the stove? Unless she didn't want to see him? He didn't like to think Jane would try to turn his daughter against him and yet…where was the girl? "Did she know I was coming?"

"Yes." Jane moved past him toward the staircase that rose from the junction of the lounge room and the study. "I'm sure she'll be back soon. Come, I'll show you the rest of the house."

Cole climbed the narrow staircase to the second floor. The worn carpet, the light falling across the banister from the window at the end of the hall, flashed him back to a winter afternoon thirteen years ago. Esther had gone to Melbourne to pick up supplies for her glazes. Jane and Cole had been out riding and had come home wet and muddy. Jane had run upstairs to change.

She was waiting for him now, at the top of the stairs, her arms crossed over her stomach. Their eyes met and hers skittered away, as if she knew the direction his thoughts had taken. Cole pushed his memories to the back of his mind where they belonged.

"This is the main bedroom, as you know." She opened the door on a room crammed with more of Esther's bric-a-brac. Jane's suitcase sat atop a cedar chest at the foot of the bed and spilled clothes onto a dark red coverlet. Hastily she stuffed bras and panties inside the case and shut the lid.

Cole left the bedroom after a brief inspection and headed next door to the bathroom. "How's the plumbing holding up?" As if on cue, the hot-water pipe started knocking.

"It's a bit dodgy," Jane admitted. "There's an ominous gurgle when you flush the toilet as if it's deciding whether to go down or up." She paused. "Do you have to mention all this to prospective buyers?"

Cole didn't answer right away; he was looking around. The avocado-green sink, toilet and bathtub, as well as the pink curtains and bath mat, had never been updated. Cole remembered peering into that speckled mirror to see if his amazing experience with Jane had changed him visibly. The wonder had been there in his eyes, but years later the scars were all on the inside.

"It's against the code of conduct for real estate agents to cover up faults in a house," Cole said, making a note on his clipboard.

He stopped in the doorway of the next bedroom and went silent. His room. Later, Jane's room. Now their daughter's things were scattered everywhere. Faded floral curtains moved in the breeze from the open window. An ancient rag rug in pink, yellow and pale blue softened the wooden floor, and a chipped white-painted dresser sat to one side. Movie posters—a decade old— still decorated the pale lavender walls. *Casablanca, Flashdance, Mad Max.*

There was the bed. High, single, virginal in white paint and a floral coverlet that matched the curtains.

Well, not quite virginal.

That afternoon he'd gone upstairs to see what was taking Jane so long. And come upon her half-dressed. There'd been a long frozen moment when their eyes met. Then her arms had dropped away from her bare breasts. He'd stepped inside the room. And shut the door. He remembered how his hands trembled and how her mouth had tasted of hot chocolate—

"There's nothing in here you haven't seen before," Jane said abruptly, moving past him out of the room.

"Mom!" a girl called. Footsteps thudded on the stairs. "The stove's broken. The egg pot boiled over, the element went *pffft* and the electricity cut out."

Mary Kate burst into the hallway. Cole dragged his mind out of the past as he looked upon the daughter he'd seen only a handful of times in his life. His heart raced as eyes uncannily similar to his own stared back at him. "Hello, Mary Kate."

"Hi." She came forward hesitantly, glancing at her mother as if for reassurance.

Cole opened his arms and took her into

a hug. Her shoulders were stiff and tense, so he kept it brief, covering his disappointment. "You've grown," he said, feeling foolishly hearty. "How tall are you now?"

Mary Kate shrugged and again looked to her mother.

"She's five feet four inches." Jane moved over to Mary Kate and put an arm around her shoulder. "She's really shot up in the past year."

Everything Cole had imagined saying to Mary Kate when they met flew out of his brain. This wasn't the warm loving reunion he'd imagined. In the face of her tepid response his own excitement fizzled. He dragged a hand through his hair and felt his scalp hot and damp. "Right, well, let's have a look at the fuse box."

The breaker was on the front veranda, so they all trooped downstairs and out into the shade of the overhanging roof. Jane peered at the faded labels above the switches until Cole edged her out of the way and flipped a switch on the top row. "That ought to do it."

"Mary Kate, go see if the stove is working," Jane said.

Mary Kate ran inside, her pink thongs flapping.

Cole waited a moment then grabbed Jane's arm and turned her to face him. "What have you been saying to her about me?"

Jane yanked her arm away. "I've never said a word against you."

"Then why won't she look at me?"

"I don't know," Jane said, pacing. "You can't expect her to be instantly affectionate. She barely knows you. A few stilted phone calls a year are no substitute for a real relationship."

"Exactly." Cole followed her along the veranda, miffed to be speaking to her back. "Whose fault is that?"

Jane spun. "Are we going to hash through this *again?* I never tried to stop you from seeing her."

"No, but you made it bloody difficult. I can understand you leaving Red Hill, but did you have to move to the other side of the ocean?"

Mary Kate ran back outside, breathless. "It's still not on. The toaster is, though, and the lights."

Cole yanked his tie loose, trying to get some breathing room. "The stove runs off a higher voltage than the toaster and kettle. You'll have to get an electrician to look at it. The house is old, it needs rewiring."

Inside, a cell phone rang. "That's mine," Jane said, and hurried away.

Alone with Mary Kate, Cole felt perspiration prickling his hairline. "So," he said. "How do you like Red Hill?"

Mary Kate twined a lock of hair around her finger and gazed at the veranda roof. "It sucks."

Unlike Jane, who only had traces of an accent, Mary Kate sounded American. She might resemble him in appearance but in all other respects she was as foreign as any stranger in the street.

"I'm really happy you're here," he plowed on. "Stephanie can't wait to see you, too. Do you remember when you were five years old and your mum brought you to Red Hill for a visit? You girls were inseparable."

Mary Kate gave him an unnerving stare. "Then why did you separate us?"

Frowning, Cole started to say, "That

wasn't my decision," then stopped. He blamed Jane, but it wasn't right to bad-mouth her to Mary Kate. All at once he couldn't handle the situation. If he stayed a moment longer his anger toward Jane would spill out and that wouldn't endear him to Mary Kate.

Stepping off the veranda, he reached into his pocket for his car keys. "Tell your mother I'll give her a call when I've worked out an asking price. I'll be in touch about you getting together with Stephanie."

JANE CAME BACK onto the veranda in time to see Cole's older-model Porsche bumping down the rutted driveway. His hasty retreat sparked a pain that hardened her resolve to get out of this town as fast as possible. He'd left their daughter standing alone on the porch looking ready to cry.

"Are you okay, sweetheart?" Jane asked, giving her a hug.

"He said he'd call you later." Mary Kate dragged a hand across her sniffly nose. "I think he's mad at me."

"No, he's not. He's mad at me." But that was no reason for him to hurt Mary Kate by taking off so abruptly.

"Come on, let's see if we can figure out what to do with that stove."

Glaring at the appliance accomplished nothing. So Jane kicked it. And immediately regretted it. Hobbling to a chair, she sat down. Cole was undoubtedly right; she needed an electrician to fix the wiring and possibly a new stove. Should she bother when she was selling? The headaches associated with disposing of her aunt's house were multiplying.

Mary Kate fished her egg out of the pot and peered at it. "This is probably as hard as a rock." She put it in a ceramic Easter-bunny egg cup. Then she got out a spoon and held the tip to the side of the shell. "He wants me to hang out with Stephanie."

"She was your best friend when you were five. For the month we were here, at least." Jane sat down again and checked her toenail. Broken. Served her right.

"What if she doesn't want to hang out with me?"

Jane shrugged helplessly, wishing she could take Mary Kate far away from these difficult encounters. It wasn't like her confident daughter to be worried about whether someone liked her. "All you can do is be yourself. I'm sure she'll love you."

Mary Kate stabbed the spoon through the shell and made a face. "Yuck. It's like rubber." Pushing it away, she sat back and asked Jane point-blank, "Why did you and Cole break up?"

"We didn't really have a choice," Jane said. "Cole asked Leslie to marry him when he found out she was pregnant. He could hardly go back on his word when he found out I was pregnant, too." Even if he'd wanted to, which he hadn't, Jane reminded herself grimly.

"But that was awful for you," Mary Kate said.

"I had big plans," Jane said briskly, refusing to tell a tale of woe. "I was going to be an actor. I couldn't do that by getting stuck in a small town. I went to Sydney and stayed with a friend of Esther's. Cole offered to send money but I refused it since he had too many people to provide for already. Esther's friend gave me free room and board in exchange for housekeeping. I was *fine*."

"So Cole stayed here and married Stephanie's mom."

"That's right." Jane sucked in a breath. She couldn't believe how much that rankled even after all these years. She'd loved Cole with all her heart and soul. He'd told her he loved her, then he'd told her he didn't. Sure, she'd wanted to be an actor but that wasn't why she'd left Red Hill; it was because Cole had chosen Leslie. The humiliation and pain had taught her a lesson—never forget, never forgive. But she kept her shoulders square and her smile bright for Mary Kate.

"That's ancient history," Jane said. "Now, are you going to eat that egg?"

"Do I have to?"

"I guess not. Put it in the fridge and we'll get something to eat in town. It's almost lunchtime, anyway. But first we'll buy a microwave. I don't know how Esther managed all these years without one."

Wonder of wonders, there was a small

appliance store in Red Hill. Jane bought a microwave and a new electric kettle to replace the one with the frayed cord. It was a miracle Esther hadn't electrocuted herself instead of dying of a heart attack.

She and Mary Kate carried their purchases back to her Mazda and stowed them in the trunk. Then they went across the street to a café with a small outdoor courtyard, its tables sheltered by market umbrellas. Jane picked up a menu and handed one to Mary Kate.

Here, in the center of town, two main roads came together in a T-junction lined by shops that made way for houses after a couple of blocks in any direction. Beyond the sparse habitation were woods broken up by rolling countryside planted with grapevines or pastureland dotted with placidly grazing sheep and cows. To the east the land rose to the promontory known as Arthur's Seat.

A comfortably round dark-haired woman in her late fifties came out of the café and stood over the table. "What can I get you ladies today?"

Jane glanced up. "Mrs. Roberts!"

"Jane Linden?" Valerie Roberts said. "Is that you?"

Jane's heart sank. She'd always believed Cole's mother didn't like her. Jane had been the outsider, the would-be usurper of Leslie's rightful place as Cole's wife.

"I'm so sorry about your aunt," Valerie went on. "Leslie and I came to the funeral but we missed paying our respects to you afterward."

"I had to rush off. My flight back to L.A. left early the next morning." And being polite to Leslie and Valerie in that difficult time would have been too much. Even now Jane's smile grew stiff. "Thank you for the flowers. They were lovely." She turned to her daughter. "This is Mary Kate. Mary Kate, this is Cole's mother. Your grandmother."

"Hi." Mary Kate eyed Valerie curiously as if trying to associate this woman with the cards she'd received like clockwork every birthday.

"It's so lovely to see you again," Valerie gushed. "My, how you've grown."

Mary Kate grimaced. "Everybody says that."

"You weren't at the funeral, were you?" Valerie asked.

"I didn't come. I had a solo in the school concert," Mary Kate explained.

"I wish I could have heard you sing." Valerie continued to study Mary Kate with embarrassing intensity. "It's been so long. Photos don't really do her justice. She's the spitting image of Cole. There's no doubt she's her father's daughter."

"Not a particle," Jane said tightly. How many boys did Valerie think she'd slept with at age seventeen? "I'd like the Thai beef salad and a latte. What do you want, Mary Kate?"

"I'll have the ham and Swiss cheese on focaccia. And a chocolate milk shake. And a piece of almond-and-orange cake for dessert."

Chuckling, Valerie jotted down their order. "A sweet tooth, just like Cole. I have to say I'm glad you're out of Los Angeles and away from that terrible smog. I worried about you and asthma."

Jane started. "How did you know she had asthma?" She'd never mentioned it to Cole for fear he'd be critical of her for staying in L.A., even though the doctors had said smog hadn't caused Mary Kate's condition.

"I didn't," Valerie said. "I was concerned because Cole had it as a child."

"I'm over it now," Mary Kate volunteered.

"Well, that's a relief." Valerie beamed at them. "I'll get your drinks right away." She glanced over Jane's shoulder. "Excuse me, someone's signaling me."

"Don't you like her?" Mary Kate asked when Valerie had hurried away. "You weren't very friendly."

"She's a nice woman. She's just so…" Jane trailed off, not wanting to taint her daughter's relationship with her grandmother. But when Jane had turned out to be pregnant, Valerie had come to Esther, and the two women had had a long discussion over what to do with her. Jane had never known anything so humiliating. As if she'd want help from the Roberts family after Cole had rejected her. "You know small towns," she finished vaguely.

Valerie came back in a few minutes with the latte and Mary Kate's milk shake. Mercifully she was busy and couldn't stop to talk.

"Mmm, this is good." Mary Kate happily slurped her milk shake through a straw.

"The coffee's not bad, either," Jane had to admit. It was as good as any in Melbourne.

A clip-clop sounded on the pavement and half a block up the road a pair of horses ridden by young girls in riding boots and hard hats walked out of the bush, crossed the road and disappeared down another trail.

Mary Kate leaned out from the table to follow their progress. "Wow! Did you see that? If we stay in Red Hill, can I get a horse?"

"What happened to your separation anxiety from the mall?" Jane asked wryly.

"That was before I knew there were horses."

"Your father has horses. You probably don't remember sitting on one when you were five." Jane added, "But we're not staying. You know that."

Valerie returned with their salad and focaccia and set the plates of food on the table. Apparently the same question was on her mind. "Will you be in Red Hill long?"

"Only as long as it takes to deal with Esther's effects and sell the farm," Jane replied.

"You're selling Cockatoo Ridge?" Hope lifted Valerie's voice. "Is Cole going to make an offer on it?"

"He's said nothing to me about that," Jane replied.

Silently, Valerie took cutlery rolled in napkins from her apron pocket and laid them beside the plates. When she spoke again she changed the subject. "I suppose you know Cole and Leslie are divorced. He has primary custody of Stephanie but he still pays Leslie a monthly sum for expenses. He helps me out occasionally and Joey's always borrowing money."

Jane spread her napkin on her lap, quietly fuming. Did Valerie think she intended to shake Cole down for child support in arrears? She'd raised Mary Kate for twelve years without asking for a cent and she had no intention of taking money from him now. Determined to put a halt to Valerie's innuendos, she said to Mary Kate, "Go wash your hands before you eat."

"But—" Mary Kate started to object.

"The washrooms are inside the café at the back," Valerie told her. Mary Kate had no choice but to leave.

Jane put down her knife and fork and looked Valerie straight in the eye. "My dealings with Cole are strictly business. He's selling the farm for me. Once that's done, Mary Kate and I are leaving and not coming back. You don't need to worry. He has no obligation to me and Mary Kate, financial or otherwise. I want *nothing* from him."

"That's not what I meant." Valerie's face fell in dismay. "I'm so sorry if you thought that."

"Then what *are* you trying to say?" Jane asked.

"Only to assure you that Cole lives up to his responsibilities. That despite his other financial obligations, he'll want Mary Kate to feel like a full-fledged part of his family." Valerie worried at the tie on her black apron. "Of course I don't mean *she's* an obligation. He's thrilled to have her back in his life. All of us—Cole, Stephanie, me, Joey, Crystal, welcome Mary Kate."

"I see," Jane said, relaxing. "That's nice."

"And you never know what will happen now that Cole and Leslie aren't together," Valerie went on, her smile returning. "You and he were fond of one another once."

Jane laughed in sheer surprise. "I can guarantee nothing will happen in that direction."

Mary Kate came back and clattered into her seat. "I'm starving."

"We'll see," Valerie said knowingly to Jane. "At any rate, I'm thrilled my grandchild has come home." She moved away, touching Mary Kate's shoulder as she went. "I'll see you *very* soon."

Jane sighed and picked up her cutlery to eat. Feeling someone's gaze on her, she glanced across the street. Cole stood in the doorway of Red Hill Real Estate, watching her.

CHAPTER THREE

WHAT THE HECK was his mother saying to Jane? Valerie meant well but she had a tendency to interfere. Cole could hardly fault her since her greatest joy was her family. He only hoped she wouldn't come across too strongly and scare Jane out of town...taking his daughter with her.

Millie summoned him to take a phone call. When he got back to the doorway, Jane was nowhere in sight; she must have gone into the café to pay. Mary Kate was about to cross the street to where Jane's Mazda was parked. She had a confident stride and seemed more grown-up than Stephanie, who was still a tomboy in many ways. It wouldn't be long before both of them were young women.

The thought tugged at him, making him

aware of how much he'd already missed. Jane clearly didn't want him to have a place in Mary Kate's life. But that was too bad. He'd spent his whole life accommodating other people. It was time to put his needs and desires first for a change. And Mary Kate was top of his priority list.

The downside was that getting to know Mary Kate would mean more contact with Jane. When she'd come into his office yesterday he'd felt the old attraction surge to the surface. It hadn't taken long before annoyance and frustration kicked in. And there was no doubt how she felt about *him*. Yet somehow they had to work together for Mary Kate's sake.

A car rounded the corner just as Mary Kate stepped off the curb, looking in the wrong direction for oncoming traffic.

Cole ran outside onto the footpath. "Mary Kate!"

She leaped out of the way and stumbled, falling to her knees on the pavement. The car swerved, narrowly missing her, and drove past, its horn blaring.

Cole ran across the road. He helped

Mary Kate to her feet and checked her over. Her knees were grazed and she was wide-eyed with the sudden fright, but that seemed the extent of her injuries. "Are you all right?"

"Yeah, I guess so." Mary Kate shivered and clutched her purse. "I'm not used to cars driving on the wrong side of the road."

"Here, the left side *is* the right side," Cole reminded her. "You've got to watch out."

Mary Kate flicked her hair behind her ears. She gave him a tentative smile. "Thanks for warning me."

"Can't let you get mowed down." Cole glanced back at the café. Jane must still be inside. "What are you and your mum up to this afternoon?"

"I guess we'll go home and sort through more of Aunt Esther's stuff. We've already got about fifty boxes of junk to throw out." Mary Kate made a face. "Not that there's much *I* can do since Mom has to look at everything first."

Cole stroked his jaw. "Do you like horseback riding?"

"Are you kidding?" Her eyes sparkled.

"I *love* it. When we were eating lunch we saw some girls ride across the street and into the woods."

"We have a couple of horses. You and Stephanie could go riding." Cole gestured toward Jane who was just coming out of the café down the street. "Go ask."

"Mom!" Mary Kate shouted, completely losing her preteen cool. "Can I go horseback riding?"

Cole waited on the corner, watching Mary Kate and Jane approach. Mary Kate was practically skipping in circles around Jane as she pleaded. Jane looked straight ahead, frowning and shaking her head.

"*Please,* can I go riding?" Mary Kate glanced toward Cole. "He said I could."

"That's right," Cole confirmed as Jane came to a halt in front of him. "My horse doesn't get enough exercise. Stephanie's always looking for someone to ride with."

"We have so much to do at the house," Jane objected. "And Mary Kate doesn't know how to ride."

"I went riding at that dude ranch in Wyoming, remember?" Mary Kate said.

"Only twice," Jane reminded her. "It's dangerous."

"We have hard hats," Cole replied. "Stephanie can ride my horse and Mary Kate can take hers. Cherry is a ten-year-old mare. She's got a smooth gait and she's very gentle." When Jane continued to hesitate, he added, "You're not going to get the house cleared out in a single weekend."

"She doesn't have the proper clothes," Jane said. "Or boots or anything."

"All she needs is a pair of long pants and sturdy running shoes," Cole countered. "We might even have a pair of Leslie's old boots that would fit her."

"*Please,* Mom?" Mary Kate begged.

Jane threw up her hands. "Oh, all right."

Mary Kate let out a whoop. "Let's go home right now so I can get changed." This time she looked right, then left, then right again before crossing the road.

"Why are you doing this?" Jane demanded of Cole.

"Do you have to ask?" He faced her square on. "She's my daughter. Stephanie's dying to see her. Besides, Mary

Kate's bored silly at the farm. I want her to be happy."

"She's happy with the way things are," Jane argued. "I don't want to complicate her life."

"There's nothing complicated about me and Stephanie. Don't you think she has a right to spend time with us?"

"She hasn't expressed much interest so far."

Cole's molars ground together. Was she deliberately goading him? Well, he wasn't going to take the bait. Taking out another business card, he scribbled his home address and phone number on the back. "Drop her off at the house. I'll call Stephanie and let her know to expect her. You can come back for her around six."

Jane slipped the card into her purse.

"Whatever my mother said to you, she means well," Cole told Jane before she could move away.

"It wasn't important."

"If it was about Mary Kate then it *is* important." Cole took a check from his breast pocket and tucked it into Jane's purse. "I know you've refused help in the past, but this is to let you know that from now on I intend to be very much in the picture when it comes to Mary Kate."

Jane pulled out the folded slip of paper, calmly ripped it in two and handed it back to him. "Do you think you can buy your way into her life? You made a choice thirteen years ago. You have to live with it. I didn't come to hit you up for child support. I don't want a cent from you."

Choice? Did she really think he'd had a choice which girl he would marry? Once he'd asked Leslie he couldn't very well have changed his mind when Jane had gotten pregnant. Especially with Leslie's family pressuring them to tie the knot. He had to live with the consequences of his actions; he accepted that. One of those consequences was that Jane distrusted him. He couldn't blame her, but…

"Does it not occur to you that it's Mary Kate you're hurting by refusing to accept money from me?" Cole said angrily. "If you think that means I don't have rights, think again. She and I are connected by blood. Nothing can break that."

Jane glared at him. "It doesn't mean you can do whatever you like with her."

Cole crumpled the torn pieces of paper in his fist. "For years I've been putting money into a trust account for her. When she's old enough, she won't need your permission to have it."

"For now, she's my responsibility and you go through me." Jane walked stiffly back to her car, head high. She got in and roared off in a spurt of gravel.

Valerie bustled across the road, still in her black apron. "She's very prickly. Are you being nice to her?"

"Yes, Mother," Cole sighed. "As nice as I can be under the circumstances. As nice as she'll allow me to be."

"We don't want to lose Mary Kate again. What are you doing about that?"

"I'm going to claim my rights to my child. Whether Jane likes it or not." He had a fleeting pang, a wish that Jane *would* like it, would like him. Then his mouth turned down. Yeah, that was going to happen. When pigs flew.

"Well, I'll leave that to you, but there's more to this situation than the child. You know what I'm talking about."

"Never mind that, Mother. The farmhouse is hers to do with as she pleases."

"I'm going to talk to her," Valerie said stubbornly. "If you won't put your own interests forward, I will." She set off across the street.

"Don't interfere. Let me deal with this," he called after her. But it was too late; Valerie was already halfway back to the café.

Cole dragged a finger around the inside of his collar. Bloody hell.

"MY HORSE KEEPS TRYING to run," Mary Kate said nervously as Cherry, the bay mare, danced along the dirt trail through the bush. She hauled on the reins with both hands and the horse's head jerked up until her neck almost touched Mary Kate's nose.

Stephanie, dressed in a pale blue T-shirt and tan jodhpurs, twisted her slender frame in her saddle to study Mary Kate's form. "Don't squeeze with your legs so hard. Cherry thinks you want her to go faster."

"But I have to hold on somehow," Mary Kate complained. "The stirrups are a lot longer than I had in Wyoming."

"Just relax," Stephanie said. "Hold on to the saddle if you have to. If you sit more loosely you'll kind of settle into the horse."

Mary Kate checked out the way the other girl sat on her horse, holding the reins in one hand and letting her legs hang in the stirrups. Taking a slow breath, Mary Kate dropped her shoulders and forced herself to relax. To her surprise and delight, Cherry immediately calmed down and fell into line behind Cole's horse, a dapple gray gelding. His name was Mr. Magoo but Stephanie said that was too long so they just called him Magoo.

They rode in silence for a while. Mary Kate snapped a sickle-shaped silver-green leaf off a branch in passing. "Pretty weird, huh, that your dad is my father, too."

Stephanie twisted around in the saddle, planting a hand on Magoo's broad silver rump. "It *is* kinda. I probably shouldn't tell you this but…sometimes he and my mum used to fight about him going out with *your* mum so soon after they'd broken up. She wasn't too happy about Dad having another daughter out there."

"I guess it would have been awkward," Mary Kate said uncomfortably.

"When it turned out that both our mothers were pregnant it was a huge mess at the time. Grammy Stanwyck tried to hush it up. She had fights with Nana Roberts, who wanted you to stay in Red Hill. Mum went along with whatever Grammy Stanwyck said. Dad was caught in the middle, just trying to do the right thing. Then your mum took off."

"How do you know all this?" Mary Kate asked, feeling sick to her stomach.

"They used to talk about it sometimes, usually at Christmas when everyone would drink too much," Stephanie said. "They didn't think I was listening, but I was."

Mary Kate fell silent, her cheeks burning with shame and rage. Everyone must hate her and her mom. Well, let them. She couldn't wait to get out of here. No wonder Mom wanted to sell up fast.

"Hey." Stephanie pulled on her horse's reins and circled around to ride side by side with Mary Kate. "Don't worry about what the grown-ups think," she said earnestly. "None of it's *your* fault. *I* think it's so cool that I've got a sister."

Mary Kate hesitated, mollified but still uncertain.

"No one mentions it nowadays, especially now that Mum and Dad are divorced," Stephanie added.

"Was that because of my mom?" Mary Kate asked.

"How could it be? She wasn't even around." Stephanie bit her lip. "I shouldn't have said anything. I didn't mean to upset you. I'm really glad you're here."

Mary Kate laughed nervously. "I always wanted a sister, too," she said, not quite able to control the tremor in her voice. "Heck, I would have been happy with a brother."

Stephanie rolled her eyes. "That's

because you don't know what they're like. Little brothers are *so* annoying." She watched Mary Kate ride for a moment then added approvingly, "You know, you *have* ridden before Wyoming. Here, when you were five."

"That's what Mom said," Mary Kate replied. "But I don't remember."

"I have a photo Dad took of both of us on the horse he owned before Magoo. We're just sitting up there bareback. I'm holding the mane, you're holding on to me."

"*I've* got a picture of you and me with ice cream cones," Mary Kate said excitedly. "The stuff is dripping all down our fronts."

"Dad has some school photos of you," Stephanie added.

"My mom doesn't have any of you," Mary Kate replied. "I wonder why."

Stephanie shrugged. "I'm not her daughter."

"But you're my sister." *Half* sister. Mom had drilled that into her. Mary Kate liked to make-believe she and Stephanie were real sisters.

Mary Kate took another deep breath, which brought with it a whiff of eucalyptus. The trees were, like, massively tall, and reminded Mary Kate of California.

"Do you miss Los Angeles?" Stephanie asked. It was almost as though she'd picked up on Mary Kate's thoughts.

"I miss my friends and going to the mall," Mary Kate said. "But Mom says there are cool boutiques in Melbourne. And now I've got you. You're lucky to have horses and be able to go riding wherever you want."

"I think *you're* lucky living in Hollywood. Did you meet heaps of celebrities?" Stephanie asked.

"We lived in Pasadena, not Hollywood. But once I went with Mom to a studio party and we saw Orlando Bloom. I got his autograph. He is so hot!"

"Wow," Stephanie breathed, her reverential tone directed as much at Mary Kate as it was at the movie star. She glanced at Mary Kate enviously. "I love your top."

"Thanks." Mary Kate glanced down at the pink T-shirt with the latest fashion logo printed across the front. *She* was jealous of Stephanie's cool black riding boots and tan jodhpurs.

"Wouldn't it be neat if you stayed in Red Hill and we could go riding all the time?" Stephanie went on.

"*I'd* like that," Mary Kate said, completely ignoring the fact that a few minutes ago she couldn't wait to leave. "But Mom wants to buy an apartment in the city."

"Maybe Dad can talk her into changing her mind," Stephanie said. "He told me he wanted us to spend time with you."

"Really? Cool. It's so weird to see my father again. I mean, I've met him before but I don't know what he's like."

Stephanie glanced over her shoulder. "Didn't your mum tell you anything about him?"

"Not much," Mary Kate admitted. "I tried to ask her a few times over the years but she got so upset—even though she pretended not to be—that I gave up."

"Doesn't she like him?"

"She *acts* like she doesn't. But before we left L.A., when she was packing and everything was out in the open, I just happened to see in her underwear drawer…" Mary Kate hesitated to tell her mother's secrets. Then again, Stephanie was her sister.

"Go on," Stephanie prompted. "What did you see?"

"A photo of Cole on a horse. He was young. The light was coming through the trees and shining on his face. He looked really handsome." Mary Kate paused thoughtfully. "I thought maybe she was keeping it to give to me someday, but when I tried to look at it, she pushed it out of sight and sent me off to finish packing my stuff."

"Wow," Stephanie said. "That's so romantic."

"It is kind of, isn't it?" Mary Kate hadn't thought of it that way before.

Stephanie glanced ahead as they emerged from bush into a meadow. "Want to race to the end of the field?"

A race? Mary Kate gulped. She didn't want to tell Stephanie she'd only cantered once before. "Sure, why not?"

With a whoop, Stephanie dug her heels into Magoo's belly. The dapple gray tore off at a gallop. Cherry leaped forward, almost jolting Mary Kate out of the saddle. She clung on, trying not to drop the reins. The wind whistled in her ears and the pounding hooves seemed to vibrate clear through to her chest. She leaned forward, low on Cherry's neck, and forgot to breathe. Magoo's gray rump was mere inches in front of Cherry's outstretched nose.

The trees on the far side of the meadow rushed closer at an alarming rate. Mary Kate started to pull back on the reins but she needn't have worried. As Stephanie slowed Magoo, Cherry automatically dropped to a canter then a trot. Mary Kate bounced lop-sidedly in the saddle, then, grinning from ear to ear, she righted herself.

"Wow! That was better than the roller coaster at Six Flags," she exclaimed.

Stephanie laughed. "Don't tell Dad we galloped. I was supposed to take it easy with you the first time."

"Can we do it again?" Mary Kate asked eagerly.

"No, we'd better walk the rest of the way," Stephanie said. "It's not far and the horses need to cool down."

Mary Kate fell in behind Stephanie as they entered a thinly wooded section where grass grew between widely spaced trees. Beyond the trees was the paddock at the back of Stephanie's house.

They came to the fence, and Stephanie leaned over and unlatched the gate, skillfully maneuvering her horse so that the gate swung open and Mary Kate could pass through on Cherry. Stephanie closed it again and they rode across the paddock to the stable. Cherry quickened her pace to a trot as she neared home. Mary Kate gripped with her thighs this time and tried to lift herself off the saddle with every step the way Stephanie did.

They came to a halt and Mary Kate flung her leg over the back of the saddle and dropped to the ground. Her legs felt all wobbly as she staggered around to the front of her horse.

"You'll be sore tomorrow, but a few more rides and you'll be fine." Stephanie looped

Magoo's reins over the fence and showed Mary Kate how to remove the saddle.

They groomed the horses and put their halters back on. Mary Kate helped carry buckets of water to fill the old bathtub that served as a water trough. Then she and Stephanie put away the saddles and bridles.

The heavy hollow clump of hooves sounded on the wooden stable floor strewn with straw as Cherry and Magoo came into their stalls looking for food. Stephanie peeled off two flakes of hay from an open bale and handed one to Mary Kate to throw into the manger for Cherry. Cherry whickered softly and bobbed her head before getting down to serious munching.

"I wish I had a horse," Mary Kate sighed, running her hand over Cherry's glossy reddish-brown neck.

"You can ride with me anytime," Stephanie offered. "Dad only rides on Sundays and even then he doesn't have time every weekend."

"Cool." Mary Kate touched Stephanie's arm as they turned to leave the stable.

"Remember what I said about that photo Mom kept in her underwear drawer? Don't say anything to your dad. Mom would have a fit if she knew I'd told you."

CHAPTER FOUR

JANE TURNED into Cole's driveway and motored slowly between rows of vines heavy with clusters of ripening grapes. Finally the house appeared; single-story cream-colored brick with a wraparound veranda and pale green roof.

She parked behind Cole's car, the older-model convertible Porsche. Interesting, the solid family man had a rakish streak. She grabbed her tote and knocked on the front door. When there was no answer she walked through the carport to the back of the house. A stable stood off to the right and beyond it was a fenced paddock. In the other corner of the yard was a concrete shed shaded by a gum tree. The door to the shed stood open.

"Hello?" Jane called, shielding her

eyes from the slanting afternoon sun. "Anyone home?"

Cole appeared in the doorway, his broad shoulders filling the space. He'd changed out of his suit into casual pants and a forest-green polo shirt that brought out the color of his eyes and showed a vee of tanned skin. "I see you found the place."

Jane walked across the short dry grass. "Where's Mary Kate? Is she ready to go?"

"They're back from their ride. But I don't know if she's ready to leave." He glanced over to the stable just as the door opened and a pair of giggling girls tumbled out. "They're getting along like a house on fire."

Mary Kate saw Jane and bounded over, beaming from ear to ear. "Mom, I had the best time. Riding is, like, brilliant! This is Stephanie."

"Hi, Stephanie. We've met but it was a long time ago."

Despite her misgivings Jane had to smile at Mary Kate's enthusiasm. With her tangled hair and grubby jeans, she looked less like a would-be Paris Hilton and more like a happy, healthy young girl. Which was wonderful, as long as she didn't get too attached to Red Hill.

"We're going to listen to music on Mary Kate's MP3 player," Stephanie said. Before either Jane or Cole could object, the girls ran toward the house.

Jane turned to Cole, one eyebrow raised. "*Brilliant?* What have you, like, done to my daughter?"

"Hey, don't blame me. I just live here." He motioned inside the shed. "I was about to open a bottle of wine. Would you care to join me for a drink?"

"I just came to pick up Mary Kate but okay, thanks," Jane said. "We do need to talk about the farm."

"Among other things." Cole led the way into the shed.

Once she was out of the sun, the temperature dropped about ten degrees. The pleasantly cool air was filled with the sweet musky scent of fermenting grapes. Shelves stacked with bottles of wine on their sides lined the back wall. A covered stainless-steel vat stood waist-high off to one side, and near it, an oval oak barrel rested on blocks. A heavy wood table held wine-making paraphernalia—beakers and thermometers and other items she didn't know the names of. Another barrel, on which two wineglasses sat upside down on a tray, provided a makeshift tasting counter.

"This is quite the hobby you have here."

"I like to experiment." He turned over the glasses and went to the fridge for a bottle of white wine. "I've got a hectare of Chardonnay and Shiraz grapes. Two years ago I put in Pinot Grigio."

There was a wistful note in his voice and he ran his hand lovingly over a row of wine-making books.

"You planned to study viticulture and own a commercial vineyard. What happened?"

Cole unscrewed the Stelvin closure and poured the wine. "I counted on taking over the farm someday. But then Dad had the car accident and died, leaving a lot of debts. My mother had no training and Joey was only a kid. When Dad's partner offered me a job at the real estate agency, I considered myself lucky."

"It's too bad. If anyone should have gotten out of Red Hill and made something out of himself, it was you," she said. "You had talent and ambition."

"What makes you think I don't still?" He handed Jane a glass. "What shall we drink to?"

"World peace?" she suggested.

He met her gaze with a wry smile. "I'd settle for détente in Red Hill."

Jane touched glasses, her glance shifting. His eyes, his smile, still had the power to make her stomach take a tumble. She held her wine up to the light coming through the doorway. It was a clear straw-yellow.

"The color will deepen to gold with age." Cole swirled the wine, put his nose inside the glass and breathed deeply.

Jane took a sip and rolled the perfumed liquid around on her tongue. "I love that buttery nutty flavor."

"That's the malolactic fermentation," Cole said. "It's out of fashion these days but I like it."

"There's fashion in wine?" Jane took another sip. "I don't know much about it but this is seriously good."

Cole tasted the wine, rolling it around in his mouth. "It's getting there."

"Don't sell yourself short." Jane picked up the wine bottle and studied the plain white sticker on which the year, the variety of grape and a catalog number was hand-written. "You could flog this at the Red Hill market. Day-tripping Melbournites would buy it by the caseload."

"Who has time for that?" he asked, leaning against the table. "Real estate agents are on the job 24-7."

"Maybe you're in the wrong job." Her cell phone rang. "Excuse me," she said, unclipping it from the side pocket of her purse. "Jane Linden speaking. Rafe, hello! Thanks for returning my call." She smiled with pleasure at hearing the gravelly two-packs-a-day voice of her old friend. "The movie premiere is in a few weeks," she told him. "Red-carpet walk at the theater. After party at the Botanical Restaurant. You put in an appearance for a couple of hours and then you can disappear. Mia will be there. Oh, don't be like that. In public you have to at least pretend to like her. *Thank* you, darling. Ciao!"

Jane folded her cell phone and tucked it into her bag. "It wouldn't do to have our male lead not show up at the Australian premiere."

"*Rafe Baldwyn?* Was that who you were talking to?" Cole said. "He's one of the hottest actors in Australia. I just read somewhere that he's going to be the next big thing in Hollywood."

"He already is," Jane said. "*Swept Away* was a smash hit in the U.S."

"Is that what your job entails, chatting with the stars?"

"Mostly I deal with the media, putting out press releases. When I arrange interviews or appearances I usually speak with agents or personal assistants. But I met Rafe years ago when he was an acting student in Sydney. We've been friends ever since."

Cole's eyebrows rose at that. "Just friends?"

"Just friends," Jane confirmed. "I was

five months pregnant, for God's sake. We met at an improv theater in Sydney. Esther's friend, the woman I was staying with, knew him, and he and I hit it off. Later, when he headed to Hollywood, I tagged along to try my luck."

"A couple of Aussies, far from home," Cole commented sardonically.

"That's right," Jane said, refusing to rise to his jibe. "Rafe's risen steadily from small parts to the top of the A-list."

"Whatever happened to *your* acting career?" Cole demanded. "You wanted to be a star, as I recall."

Jane twirled her glass by the stem, avoiding his gaze. "I got a couple of decent roles but in the end, nothing came of it."

"I don't understand," Cole persisted. "You were very talented. The hit of the high school play."

"I was a big fish in a small pond."

"But you wanted it so badly."

"What do you care? It's ancient history." Changing the subject, she asked, "Have you had a chance to put a value on the farm?"

"That depends." Cole sipped his wine. "If you're willing to hold out for what the land is worth, you could probably get a million for it. But if you're after a quick sale I'd suggest asking eight hundred, maybe eight hundred and fifty thousand. If you fix the plumbing and wiring it might sell faster."

"Fixing things takes time," Jane objected. "I don't want to wait for major repairs. List the property as is for one million."

"Okay. You can always come down if it's not selling." Cole swirled the last of his wine and drained it. Then he set his glass on the barrel and straightened as if getting down to the *real* business at hand. "Now, about Mary Kate."

Jane stiffened, her fingers curling tightly around the stem. "What about her?"

"I want a definite arrangement between us, something binding, about when I can see her."

Jane felt herself go cold all over. "Are you talking about a legal arrangement?"

"Yes. Joint custody. How do I know

you won't up and disappear across the Pacific again?"

"I didn't return to Australia because Esther died," Jane said. "I was planning on coming home anyway. Mary Kate's at a transitional age and I think Melbourne is a saner and safer environment than where we lived in L.A."

Red Hill was even better in that respect than Melbourne, but she'd be crazy to put herself through the anguish of seeing Cole on a regular basis. Not that she *cared,* but he was a constant reminder of the unhappiness he'd caused her in the past. And though she hated to admit it, he still had something that attracted her.

"It's going to be difficult—" Jane began.

"Even so, I want something binding," Cole said, cutting her off. "The girls are fast friends already. If you discourage Mary Kate from seeing Stephanie it could set off consequences you may not like."

"Consequences?" she repeated, alarm bells ringing. "Is that a threat?"

"Just a suggestion to consider everyone's feelings," he said with a grim smile. "I got the feeling you expected to blow into town and out again without causing a ripple in any of our lives."

That was exactly what she'd hoped to do. Clearly it wasn't going to work. Stalling, she said, "Why don't we ad-lib while I'm in Red Hill? When I move back to the city we can hammer out something more concrete."

"As long as you understand I'm not going away. I've had a chat with my lawyer about my custody rights."

The phrase pushed Jane close to panic. She wasn't a clinging mother, but Mary Kate was all she had. Already her daughter was growing up, growing away from her. Add a father, a new sister, horses—and a lawyer—how could she compete? "I suppose she could come out occasionally on weekends," Jane said reluctantly. "But I'm not sure she would like being away from me."

"I've got room here for guests," Cole replied.

The thought of staying overnight in his house brought heat surging to her cheeks.

"Oh, sure, like that would work," she scoffed. "You and I under one roof?"

"I'm willing to do anything for my daughter."

Was he suggesting she wouldn't? "While I appreciate the offer, no thank you." She set her empty glass on the wine barrel and started toward the door. "It's getting close to dinnertime and I don't want to hold you up. Mary Kate and I need to get going."

Cole stopped her with a hand on her forearm. "You told your friend Rafe he had to pretend to like Mia. We need to at least pretend to like each other. For our daughter's sake."

Though his hand burned her skin, his words were like a wash of cold water. The old days truly were gone. She was nothing more to him than an annoying impediment to his relationship with his daughter.

"We have a daughter together," Cole said, his voice softening fractionally. "I don't want us to be enemies."

How could they be friends when he was trying to take her baby away from her?

"I'm sure we can work things out," she said stiffly, adding, "Our relationship has to be strictly business."

"Fine," he said, his voice tight. "Business, it is."

Even though she was pushing him away as hard as she could, deep inside, a tiny piece of Jane's heart chipped. Funny, she hadn't thought there was anything left to break. "Excellent. I'm glad we understand each other."

SHOWING PROSPECTIVE customers around Cockatoo Ridge filled Cole with a peculiar mixture of pride, longing and bitterness. He knew exactly where the daffodils his grandmother had planted around the grassy lawn would peek through in early spring. He knew where the veranda deck had been repaired after he'd backed the utility truck into it while learning to drive. If he was very quiet he could almost hear the lambs bleating. Except that they'd been gone for fifteen years now.

The farm was in his bones and in his blood. As a ten-year-old he'd imagined he

would always live here. Now, as a thirty-
one-year-old, it was still where he wanted
to put down roots. Gazing out over the
valley he could picture grapevines growing
in long neat rows, down to the creek, then
up the other side of the hill. But he would
plant around the massive old gum tree
where the sulfur crested cockatoos that gave
the farm its name nested in the hollow trunk.

"Cole, dear?" Audrey O'Keefe appeared
at his elbow, resplendent in a fuchsia
blouse worn over emerald pants. She and
her husband, Bert, had followed him from
the office in their car. "How many acres
did you say were here?"

Cole emerged from his reverie to focus
on the woman who captained his mother's
lawn-bowling team. Audrey wore chunky
rings on every finger, and a pair of oversize
sunglasses perched in a nest of bright
orange hair. As if to compensate for her
gaudiness, her husband, Bert, wore plain
brown shorts and a beige shirt. His
thinning hair was a nondescript shade
somewhere between pale blond and gray.

"Five hectares or about ten acres in the

old measure," Cole said as he led the couple to the house. "The house was built by my grandfather in the 1800s. But you know that."

The O'Keefes were the fifth couple he'd shown the house to that week. So far he hadn't gotten even a nibble and he wasn't expecting one today. Audrey and Bert were so different it was hard to please both.

"It's gorgeous," Audrey said as Cole rang the doorbell. "I've always loved the Victorian trim on the veranda."

"Are the plumbing and wiring up to code?" Bert asked.

Jane opened the door. In a pale pink top over a white denim skirt she looked as cool and sweet as peppermint ice cream. His impulse as a man was to try to charm her. But that was not on. If she wanted a business relationship, that's exactly what she was going to get.

He nodded to her formally then answered Bert's question. "There was no code when this place was built, and the plumbing and wiring are original. They'll need complete redoing before the place is livable."

Jane's mouth dropped open as if she couldn't believe what she was hearing. He couldn't blame her, he supposed. He'd just told potential buyers that her house needed tens of thousands of dollars of repair.

"Bert and Audrey O'Keefe," Cole said. "Jane Linden."

"Come in, please," Jane said, opening the door wider.

"I was sorry to hear your aunt passed on, darl'." Audrey patted Jane's arm. "So sad."

Jane's smile for the O'Keefes turned to a glare for Cole as the couple passed into the hall. Cole was about to follow, when she snagged his suit sleeve. "What are you doing telling them about the plumbing and wiring?"

Cole smoothed out the fabric of his suit. "I told you, I can't conceal structural faults from clients."

"Look at those ceiling roses!" Audrey's voice carried from the lounge room. "What do you think, Bert? Wouldn't this big old house be perfect for when the grandkids come to visit?"

"The plumbing isn't up to scratch," Bert reminded her as he trailed after her into the kitchen.

Jane threw her hands in the air. "If you've mentioned the plumbing and wiring to every prospective buyer, it's no wonder no one's made an offer."

"I thought you were going back to Melbourne on Sunday," Cole said. "It's Thursday and you're still here."

"There's too much to do," Jane replied. "I decided I'd just go in for meetings as necessary."

"Lovely big kitchen," Audrey boomed as she sailed back into the lounge room with Bert in her wake.

"Linoleum's peeling," Bert said gloomily.

"Mind if we look upstairs?" Audrey said, ignoring her husband. "How many bathrooms?"

"One and a half," Jane said.

"Bert gets the half." Audrey jabbed him with her plump elbow and brayed laughter. "Oh, what the hell, darl', we'll build you a shower, too."

Bert trudged up the narrow staircase

behind his wife. "You know we can't afford to renovate."

"Audrey is a good friend of my mother's," Cole explained to Jane in a low voice. "I definitely can't lie to her."

"Nobody's asking you to lie," Jane replied. "But you could wait until they ask before you point out the defects of the house."

"I have to live in this town," Cole said. "I have a reputation for honesty and integrity. How could I stay in business if I concealed or glossed over faults? More to the point, how could I live with myself? My father always told me, all a man has is his reputation. When that's gone, there's nothing left."

"Pretty rich, coming from a man who gambled away his family home."

Cole tightened his jaw, controlling his temper. "Next time, perhaps you should arrange to be out when I show people around."

"So you can say even worse things about my house?" Jane shook her head as she paced between the dining table and the back of the couch. "You—"

She broke off as Audrey descended the stairs, loudly declaring, "I like the rose-patterned wallpaper. It's that—what do you call it?—shabby chic."

"More like, shabby shi—"

"*Bert,*" Audrey cut him off. She emerged into the lounge room, and seeing Jane and Cole, smiled broadly. "Thanks for letting us view your house, darl'. This place has heaps of potential."

"Wait for me at the bottom of the driveway and you can follow me to the next house," Cole instructed Bert. As the O'Keefes walked out to their car, he explained to Jane, "I'll report back later with the O'Keefes' impressions."

"Oh, I don't think that's necessary. I can already tell how it went." She followed him onto the veranda. "You're not doing your best to sell this place for a million dollars, are you? I think you're trying to drive the price down so you can pick it up cheaply."

Cole froze. Slowly he turned, trying to hold on to his temper. Yes, he would like to have the farm, but to be accused of sabotage… "You should know me better than that."

She crossed her arms over her chest. "I know you're capable of lying. You lied to me thirteen years ago."

That stopped him short. He couldn't deny it, even though the lie he'd told wasn't what she thought it was. His jaw set, he stepped off the veranda and walked toward his car without another word.

"Cole! What time should I pick up Mary Kate?"

Fists curled, he kept his voice even. "Stephanie asked her to stay for dinner."

"Again?" Jane frowned. "No, she's spending too much time there. I want her home."

A slow burn started deep in his belly. Was she going to withhold access to Mary Kate to punish him for what he'd said about the house? In spite of his hard line regarding access to Mary Kate, he'd hoped they could come to a reasonable agreement concerning their daughter, but maybe that wasn't possible.

"Fine. You can pick her up at six o'clock."

Later that afternoon, when he got back to the office, he put through a call to his lawyer. "Ron, remember what we talked about regarding Mary Kate? Go ahead and send that letter of intent. I want to get the ball rolling."

He hung up. He hated that he and Jane were fighting over Mary Kate. Especially when he could still recall what they used to mean to each other; how he made her laugh. How she made him tremble. A hollow ache formed in his gut. Things could have been so different for them.

CHAPTER FIVE

JANE PRESSED her cell phone to her ear, waiting for Mia to pick up, while she watched the cup of instant noodles spin in the microwave.

She was about to give up and click off her phone when Mia MacDonald finally answered sleepily. "Hello?"

"Mia!" The microwave dinged. Jane searched frantically among the boxes of packed-up dishes and pantry contents for a pot holder. "I want to tell you about the premiere."

"Can't make it, darling," Mia said in a bored drawl. "I'll be on a yacht in Bora-Bora."

Jane found the oven mitts under the phone book and slipped them on. "Gee, that's too bad. Rafe is dying to see you. He specifically asked if you were coming." So he could avoid her, but Mia didn't need to know that.

"Oh?" Mia perked up. "What did he say exactly?"

Jane had heard all the gossip from the set about how Mia had it bad for Rafe but Rafe wasn't interested. "He thinks you're a hottie."

"Well, I know *that*," Mia purred and Jane could just imagine her curling self-satisfied smile. Then her voice turned petulant. "But his girlfriend is so possessive. She's always hanging around, getting in our way."

"I heard rumors they were breaking up." *Sorry, Rafe.* Opening the microwave door, Jane tucked the phone under her cheek and reached for the cup of noodles. "Colette Dinnigan offered to make you a dress especially for the premiere," Jane added her final incentive.

"Ooh, I love her sparkly designs," Mia cooed then immediately demanded, "What about jewelry? I want diamonds. They look so nice against my dark hair."

These were tasks for Mia's PA. But Mia

didn't care who did the running around as long as she got what she wanted.

"I can get you diamonds," Jane promised recklessly, carefully setting the overflowing noodles on top of the phone book. "Anything else?"

"I'm not a diva like some people—"

"Mia, you're a star."

"I am, aren't I? Just the usual—Bolly and caviar. Russian, of course. I won't eat anything else."

"Naturally," Jane agreed, privately convinced that a girl from Woop Woop wouldn't know Russian caviar from sea urchin roe. "So I can count on you to be there?"

"Darling, I wouldn't miss it! Give Rafe my love."

Jane hung up and made notes on a pad of paper. Diamonds. Colette Dinnigan. Champagne and caviar. Mia MacDonald was high maintenance. Standing amid the clutter of half-packed boxes, Jane was forking noodles into her mouth when the doorbell rang. Tossing the half-finished cup into the bin, she went to open it.

"Valerie!" Jane said, taken aback. "I didn't expect to see you again so soon."

Valerie presented her with a deli foil tray and a hunk of cake wrapped in plastic. "Lasagna, from the café. I heard your stove isn't working. The cake is for Mary Kate. She seemed to enjoy it so much the other day."

"Thank you. That's really kind. Um, would you like to come in?" Jane stepped back and opened the door wider.

Valerie's gaze drifted over Jane's shoulder. "If I'm not interrupting anything."

"Not at all." Jane led the way down the hall. "Have a seat. I'll put these in the fridge. Do you want coffee?"

"Nothing for me, thanks." Valerie gravitated to the window looking out over the valley.

She was still there when Jane returned from the kitchen. "How I miss this view. I came here as a bride, left as a widow." Sighing, she turned. "It should have belonged to Cole. Not that I blame anyone but my husband, God rest his blasted soul."

Jane perched on the edge of a chair, gripping her hands in her lap. "Where do you live now?"

"A little house in town. I don't need much these days." Valerie sat opposite on the couch and gazed around at the dingy green walls. "Before Jake died and we had to sell, I'd planned to paint this room a lovely cream color. Would have brightened it right up."

"Aunt Esther was more interested in her pottery than anything else." Which reminded her, she needed to put an ad in the paper to sell the kiln and the wheel.

Valerie glanced around. "Is Mary Kate here?"

"She's riding with Stephanie. She won't be home for a few hours."

"That's fine. I really wanted to talk to you, anyway."

"Oh?" Jane said warily.

"You know, you didn't follow the plan Esther and I set out for you," Valerie told her with a small smile. "We had it all figured out. You were supposed to have your baby in Sydney with Esther's friend then come back to Melbourne where we could see you and Mary Kate often."

Jane lifted a shoulder, uncomfortable. "I had an opportunity to go to L.A. so I took it. Esther knew I wanted to act."

"You took my grandchild overseas." Valerie's tremulous voice was faintly accusing. "Did you know I offered to raise her myself since you were so bent on pursuing an acting career?"

"Esther told me. She offered, too." Jane gripped her fingers, recalling the pressure she'd been under to do what everyone told her would be best for her child. When she thought of those early days now, she shuddered at her foolhardy confidence in blithely setting off for Los Angeles as a single mother with a baby. Too young to know better, she'd managed with the help of Rafe and his cousin, Linda, who had a young family and didn't mind babysitting one more child occasionally. "Mary Kate was my daughter. I couldn't give her up then." And she wouldn't give her up now.

"No, of course not." Valerie blinked, her

tight smile crooked at the corners. "Anyway, that's not what I'm here about."

Jane waited, expecting a reprise of Valerie's café speech about how wonderful it was for Mary Kate to be reunited with Cole's family.

"I know you're planning on selling the farm," Valerie said. "But I would like you to consider Cole when you make your plans."

"I understand that he wants Mary Kate nearby, but I need to live in Melbourne for my work," Jane replied. And to stay as far as possible away from Cole.

"You misunderstand me," Valerie said. "I do wish Mary Kate would be living closer. But I'm confident Cole will have her stay with him often. No, I didn't come here to try to change your mind about moving."

"Then why did you come?" Jane was genuinely mystified.

"To ask you to sell the farm back to Cole for a reasonable price. He can't afford a million dollars. When your aunt bought Cockatoo Ridge she paid a fraction of that. Land prices were a fifth of what they are now, plus we had to let it go cheap because we were, to put it mildly, desperate."

"I don't know what to say." Jane shook her head, stunned. "I have plans for the money. I need it to purchase the apartment I want in the city."

"Just think about it," Valerie urged. "You owe Cole, don't you think?"

"*Me,* owe *him?*" Jane tossed her hair. She eyed Valerie narrowly. "Did Cole put you up to this?"

"Oh, no," Valerie said placatingly. "He has no idea I'm here. He'd be extremely upset if he knew I'd suggested such a thing to you."

"I hope so," Jane replied.

Valerie rose. "Look, I don't want to pressure you. I just hope you'll think about it. It's not just Cole you need to consider. There's also Mary Kate. This farm is her heritage as much as Stephanie's."

Silently, Jane fingered her necklace of long strands of freshwater pearls while her anger grew. She did not need this guilt trip. Yet she would do well to pay attention to what Valerie was saying. While she'd been thousands of miles away on another continent it had been easy to convince herself that Cole and his family were nothing to her and Mary Kate. Now she was face-to-face with reality, forced to confront difficult issues she'd ignored for too long. It wasn't just Cole who wanted to take Mary Kate away from her. His family had a claim, as well.

"You probably think I have no right to ask this of you," Valerie went on when Jane didn't speak. "But mothers fight for their children."

Stephanie as a sister and best friend, Cole for a father, Valerie as the loving grandmother, combined with this wonderful old farmhouse and plenty of land to ride horses. It was too much for Jane to compete against. Why would she make it easy for Cole to lure Mary Kate away from her?

"Yes, we do fight for our children," Jane replied tightly. "That's why I will not sell for less than full market price."

IF HE SOLD his house, cashed in his retirement fund, liquefied his portfolio, borrowed the maximum, and *if he sold the multimillion-dollar Rasmussen estate and got a big fat commission,* he just might be able to put down enough cash to keep the monthly mortgage repayments manageable.

Cole threw his pen down, discouraged. Jane was wrong in thinking he was deliberately trying to drive down the price of Cockatoo Ridge—he would never do anything like that—but she'd been right about his wanting to buy it for himself.

Well, he had to start somewhere and selling the Rasmussen estate was the best way to get the money train rolling. He picked up the phone and dialed a Melbourne businessman he'd shown through the estate a couple of weeks previously. "G'day, Anthony. How's it going? Thought I'd give you a hoy to see if you've changed your mind about the Rasmussen property. Another look might— Oh, is that right? Congratulations. Let me know if I can help you in the future."

Cole hung up and paged through his client list. There weren't many people who could afford an estate with an asking price of over eight million dollars.

Joey came out of his office and stood in Cole's doorway. "I couldn't help overhearing. The Rasmussen estate needs to be marketed to a clientele with serious money."

"My brother, the expert. For your information, Anthony is an investment banker. He's not interested because he just bought a mansion in Toorak." Cole took a brown bag out of his bottom drawer and unwrapped a ham-and-cheese sandwich. "Speaking of money, have you got that three hundred you owe me?" Joey's wages had gone straight from the firm's account into his personal bank account yesterday, so Cole knew he had the bucks.

"Sorry, mate. Not this week. Soon, though. I promise."

"What happened to your paycheck?"

Joey didn't answer. His fingers twitched at his side.

"For crying out loud, Joey!" Cole crumpled his lunch bag and tossed it at the wastebasket. "If you keep playing the slot machines you'll never get out of debt.

Look at the problems Dad's gambling caused for our family. You don't want that for you and Crystal. Call the help line. Get some counseling."

"I don't have a problem. I've just had a run of bad luck lately. I'll sort it out." A crooked smile split Joey's face. With the dark cowlick falling over his forehead, he reminded Cole of their father. Jake had wheedled his way around Valerie, just as Joey was trying to do to Cole. "Don't mention this to Crystal, okay?"

Furious, Cole sat back in his chair. "You don't think she'll notice?"

In the outer office a woman cleared her throat. Millie, Cole knew, had gone to lunch.

"I've got to show a house in two minutes," Joey said, glancing at his watch. With that he went out the back door to the car park.

"I'm surprised you haven't strangled him yet," Jane said from the doorway.

Cole, who'd started to rise, sank back into his chair. Great, just the person he needed to witness Joey being an idiot. "I'm trying to restrain myself long enough for him to grow up."

Cole had only seen Jane briefly a handful of times since the day he'd shown Audrey and Bert the house. While neither had backed down over the house or Mary Kate, relations between them had become more or less civilized. The difficulty was, he liked being around Jane. And he was far from immune to her dark blue eyes, her slender, graceful hands and her throaty laughter.

She sat in the chair Joey had vacated and crossed her smooth, tanned legs. One sandal dangled by a thin glittery strap from manicured toes. Her fingers played with her beads, drawing his eye back up to the deep V neckline of her softly draped blouse.

"He'll never do that if you treat him like a child and keep covering his mistakes," Jane said.

Cole adjusted his tie and sat straighter, as if he could, by his posture, counteract the sensual way she lounged in his guest chair. "I hope you didn't come to lecture me on child rearing."

"I came to get the names of those tradesmen," she said. "My vision of a quick sale is rapidly disappearing. If fixing the place up will help, I'll try it."

Cole leaned back in his chair and twiddled a pencil in his fingers. "It's been two weeks with nary a nibble. Do you want to drop the price?"

"No," she said decisively. "I want the full amount."

Cole reached for his cardholder and began flipping through the overstuffed pewter box. "William Lasky is a local guy. And an excellent electrician."

"I remember William," Jane mused. "Short guy with braces."

"He's matured since ninth grade," Cole said. "If I tell him it's a rush job he'll pull out all the stops. I also know a first-rate plumber who won't overcharge you." Cole found the cards he was looking for and wrote the contact details on a memo pad. Handing her the paper, he said, "Tell William I sent you."

Jane held the paper without speaking.

"Was there something else?" Cole asked.

"Your mother came to see me."

Cole dragged a hand across his face.

"I'm sorry about that. She can't help inter-
fering. Don't listen to a word she says."

"I wasn't planning to." Jane tucked the
memo paper in her purse. She rose and
paused to search his face. "I hope she was
telling the truth when she said you had
nothing to do with her visit."

Cole frowned. Before he could puzzle
that out, girlish giggles erupted in the
hallway. A pair of young faces peered
through the crack in the door.

"What are you two doing here?" Cole
asked. "Where are the horses?"

"We left them across the road in
Jackson's back garden," Stephanie said. "I
came to borrow a few bucks to get Mary
Kate and me ice cream cones."

"Everyone thinks I'm made of money,"
Cole grumbled and pulled his wallet out of
his back pocket. "Here's five. Bring me
back the change."

"Thanks." Stephanie slid the money into
the front pocket of her jeans. She made no
move to leave.

"What else?" Cole demanded, pretending to be stern.

Stephanie glanced at Mary Kate, who nudged her in the ribs and set them both to giggling again. Laughter making her voice wobble, Stephanie said, "I told Mary Kate the ice cream at Arthur's Seat is the best. Can you take us?"

"In case you hadn't noticed, this is the middle of a workday."

"Mom, can you take us?" Mary Kate asked.

"I would but the backseat is full of boxes for the rubbish tip," Jane told her.

"Please, Dad?" Stephanie begged. "It's still lunchtime. She came around his desk to open his appointment book. "When's your next showing?"

"Not until four-thirty." He paused, then relented. "Oh, all right. Let's go."

"Are you coming, Mom?" Mary Kate asked. "You've *got* to come. Please?"

Jane glanced uncertainly at Cole.

Cole shrugged, trying to appear as if it made no difference to *him* if she joined them. "The girls would like it. Why not come along?"

"Yay!" Mary Kate and Stephanie bounced

up and down. "We're all going for ice cream!"

Cole threw an amused glance at Jane. "Approximate age, seven?"

"That might be pushing it," she replied above the girls' clamor. "What about the horses?"

"Jackson said we could leave them as long as we like," Stephanie told her. "He wants them to eat down the grass."

The bell over the entrance dinged as Millie returned from lunch. Cole went to tell her he was going out for a while, then led Jane and the girls to where the Porsche was parked.

The girls crawled over the folded passenger seat and squashed into the tiny rear seat. Jane climbed into the front. What she was thinking? Just being jammed in this small car so close to Cole made her nervous. She tugged on the seat belt and failed to get it to release. There was no way she could call eating ice cream strictly business, but she didn't see how she could back out now. Damn belt. What was wrong with it?

"Everyone strapped in?" Cole called

over the back of his seat. Having received affirmation from that quarter, he glanced at Jane. "Having trouble?"

She blew her bangs out of her eyes and glared at him from under her lashes. "I'll get it."

"Let me." Cole reached across her for the belt.

Jane sucked her stomach in, a vain attempt to shrink away from his hands. Knuckles brushed her rib cage, fingers nudged her hip, as he pulled the two ends together. Color rushed to her cheeks and wildfire spread along her nerves.

With a click he pushed the buckle into place. His eyes met hers. "A slow smooth action usually gets results."

Jane laughed even as her face burned. "Aunt Esther used to warn me about cars and boys. Are we going for ice cream, or not?"

"Ice cream!" came the chorus from the backseat.

Cole started the engine and pulled onto the narrow, eucalypt-lined road that led along the ridge toward the mountaintop. Jane sat with her knees together, her hands clasped in her lap. Cole's hand on the gearshift was so close it occasionally brushed her skirt. As he worked the clutch his thigh muscles strained against the cloth of his pants.

Jane turned to the window to watch the passing countryside instead of Cole. It was crazy and dangerous to notice him this way when they were so at odds over Mary Kate and the house. When she wasn't mad at him, she came too darn close to liking him. *Really* liking him. Vineyards fell away down the hill on either side and farm buildings gradually gave way to houses as they neared the summit.

Ten minutes later they were at the top of Arthur's Seat Park. Tourist buses chugged slowly past the giant-size iron chair that gave the park its name. Cole pulled into a parking spot overlooking the curving bay with the Melbourne skyline hazy in the distance.

Stephanie pulled out the five-dollar bill and scrambled from the car. "Mary Kate and I will get our own ice cream."

Cole and Jane followed them to the kiosk next to the restaurant. When the girls had their ice cream and had run off to look through the telescope trained across the bay, Cole asked Jane, "What would you like?"

She shrugged. "Any flavor will do."

"The Jane Linden I used to know would have spent half an hour choosing between five of her favorites." He ordered two cones with double scoops of Rocky Road.

"I see you have a taste for irony." She licked a swathe around the softening mound of ice cream.

"We're sharing ice cream," he said. "Things could be worse."

Cole strolled toward the railing along the cliff edge and leaned on it, contemplatively eating his cone. The girls, achingly young and innocent, swiveled the telescope around to different landmarks. They shrieked with laughter, their hair blowing in the wind. Jane followed more slowly. To an outsider, she and Cole must look like a married couple with their two daughters.

"They could be better, too, though," Cole said when she'd joined him.

"How so?" Jane asked.

"Stephanie and Mary Kate could have been enjoying each other's company all through their childhood. I could have seen Mary Kate's first steps, dropped her off on her first day at school, taught her to ride a horse…"

"Oh, really?" Jane's gut twisted around the cold lump of ice cream she'd just swallowed. "And *Leslie* wouldn't have had something to say about that?"

"Don't pretend this is only about Leslie," Cole said. "You told me over and over that term break how you couldn't wait to get out of Red Hill."

"I wanted to see the world, to do something with my life. I'd watched so many people leave high school and never go anywhere." Too late she realized what she'd said. "Oops."

Cole's cone cracked. "Are you referring to me?"

"No, don't be silly. You may have stayed in Red Hill but you've built a successful business." Jane winced inwardly. She must have struck a nerve with Cole.

"What exactly have you been telling Mary

Kate about me all these years?" he demanded, ignoring her hasty backpedaling.

"You spoke to her on the phone plenty of times," Jane said. "She knew who you were, what you were about."

"Yes, but what did *you* say?"

"I told her you were a boy I'd known in high school. We didn't get married because you were already engaged. A couple of times I tried to talk about her feelings about growing up without her father around. She was uncomfortable with the subject so I don't like to bring it up."

"Odd, don't you think?" Cole said. "Wouldn't a girl be curious about her father? What did she say to her friends when they asked where I was?"

"I don't know," Jane began then remembered something. "There was one time when she was about seven. She told her school friend that her father was an important diplomat in Bangkok. Don't ask me how she knew about diplomats. Maybe she saw it on TV."

"Did you correct her and tell her I was a real estate agent?"

"Not in front of her friend." Jane shook her head in exasperation. "Is there any point in this discussion?"

"I want to know why she felt she had to make up stories about me." Cole kicked at a stone and sent it skittering across the pavement. "Were you embarrassed because I was the small-town boy you left behind? The guy who never made anything of himself? Did that attitude rub off on your daughter? Is that why Mary Kate invented an important job for me?"

"Come on, Cole. You know it wasn't like that." Jane felt a sudden surge of anger. "I would never have left if you hadn't dumped me to marry Leslie. I wanted to become an actor, yes, but I'd hoped we could plan a future together. You made your choice. Now you have to live with the consequences. *You don't get to be the most important person in Mary Kate's life.*"

"A child needs a mother *and* a father," he said evenly, but there was a steely edge to his voice. "I need to make up for lost years. Tomorrow I want to spend the day with Mary Kate, just her and me."

CHAPTER SIX

So Cole wanted time with Mary Kate. Well, fine. Jane could handle that. Consulting the pancake recipe, she poured the liquid ingredients into the flour mixture and quickly beat them together. As long as all parties clearly understood that *she* was Mary Kate's mother and that her daughter lived with *her.*

Joint custody. The very term struck terror in Jane's heart. Maybe she was being foolish and unrealistic to think she could keep her daughter all to herself forever. But it wasn't only about losing Mary Kate. Those moments in the car when she'd responded to Cole's presence had set alarm bells ringing. Once he was in their lives she would be thrown together with him constantly. Seeing him didn't just remind her of why she hated him, but also of why she'd fallen in love with him.

"What are you making?" Mary Kate shuffled over to peer into the mixing bowl. Her hair was uncombed and her pajama sleeves grazed her knuckles.

"Your favorite. Pancakes." Jane's heart turned over, realizing her daughter's head was nearly level with hers. When had that happened?

Mary Kate tasted a dab of batter and wrinkled her short straight nose. Bunching her fists inside her sleeves, she looked at Jane. "What were you and Cole talking about yesterday at the park? It looked pretty intense."

Jane stirred briskly, whisking the batter so hard it swirled a hollow in the middle. "We were discussing the past. He wishes he'd had more time with you, growing up."

"I always wondered why you couldn't, like, work things out," Mary Kate said. "You said once that my father was the love of your life."

"Did I?" Jane froze. When had she said that and what had possessed her to make such a revelation? She looked down and discovered she'd beaten all the lumps out of the batter. Tough pancakes coming up.

"Mom, why does it bother you so much to talk about him?"

"Me?" Jane said. "I thought it was you." In spite of what Cole thought, Jane didn't want Mary Kate to think badly of him, so she'd never told her daughter how deeply she'd been hurt. "It *is* hard for me to talk about him."

Mary Kate went to the fridge for orange juice and poured them both a glass. "So, *was* he the love of your life?"

Jane sighed, remembering a summer morning and a boy on a horse. "Did I ever tell you how we met?"

"No, tell me now."

"I noticed him in high school, but we never had much to do with each other. He hung out with the sporty crowd. I was with the arty types. And, you know the saying, never the twain shall meet. Until one day…" Jane turned on the electric frying pan she'd found in the pantry. "I was walking down by the creek when

Cole came along on his horse, a big chestnut gelding.

"I nodded and expected he would ride on by. Instead, he reached into his shirt pocket and showed me a baby possum he'd found at the base of a tree that had fallen out of its mother's pouch."

"Oh, poor thing," Mary Kate said. "What happened?"

"We went up to the farm and I found an old shoe box. We lined it with leaves and put the possum inside. Cole handled the baby animal so gently I remember looking at his hands and thinking…" She pulled herself up. "Well, anyway, we talked my aunt into driving us to the vet."

"Did the possum survive?"

Jane nodded. "A few weeks later we released it back where Cole had found it." She tested the heat of the pan with a drop of water, watching it sizzle away to nothing. "It's funny. Until that day, when he walked into this house and went straight to the kitchen where I'd said there was a box, I hadn't known Cockatoo Ridge had been his family home. It must have been hard for him, seeing us living there."

"Was that when you two started going out?"

"Not on dates, per se," Jane replied. "My aunt had a horse that she encouraged me to ride to get me outside instead of always watching movies. I never enjoyed it much on my own. But the next Saturday when Cole rode up to the house and asked if I wanted to go with him, well, I didn't say no. After that, we were together every chance we could get. We were on break between school terms, so that was pretty often."

"Did you love him?"

Jane poured batter into the pan in four neat circles. "Yes, I loved him," she said quietly. "I thought he loved me, too. But he didn't."

Mary Kate fell silent. After a minute, she asked, "Or was it *me* he didn't love?"

"No, sweetheart," Jane said, dismayed. "When he married Leslie he didn't even know you."

"Is that why you went so far away, to cure your broken heart?"

The moon wouldn't have been far enough away for that. But she was reluctant to admit to Mary Kate how much Cole had hurt her, so she fell back on her standard explanation. "I had ambitions. If you're going to be an actor, you can't stay in a small town." Jane studied Mary Kate's somber expression. "Are you angry with me for not making sure you saw your father more?"

The girl shrugged but made no reply.

"I'm sorry." Bubbles were forming rapidly in the batter and she turned the heat down. "You're all I have, honey. I didn't want to lose you."

Mary Kate laughed incredulously. "I'm your daughter. How could you lose me?"

So many ways, it wasn't funny. Jane flipped the pancakes. "Breakfast is ready. Can you get plates?"

Mary Kate went to the cupboard for dishes and Jane slid the pancakes onto them. Thoughtfully, Jane asked, "Do you remember when you were in grade two? You told Lisa from your class that your father was a diplomat in Bangkok."

Mary Kate scrunched up her face as she sank into a chair at the table. "Oh, God, I'd forgotten. But yes, I did."

Jane spooned fresh strawberries on top of her pancakes. "What were you thinking then? I'm just curious."

Mary Kate slathered on butter and syrup. "That I didn't want to look like a loser whose own father didn't want to know her."

"Oh, honey." Jane set aside the bowl of strawberries. Despite Mary Kate's lighthearted assurance that she couldn't lose her, Jane knew her fears weren't so far-fetched. Yet if she tried to keep Mary Kate from Cole the situation could worsen. And Mary Kate deserved to know her father. "Cole's been after me all week to let you spend time with him. Yesterday he said he wanted to take you somewhere today, just the two of you."

"Yeah?" Mary Kate brightened. "What did you say?"

"I said I'd ask you. It's…all right with me. After breakfast you can call him."

"Do you think Stephanie will mind?"

"Don't worry about that. I'm sure Cole has talked to her."

"But what's going to happen? Am I going to live with him part-time?"

Jane stopped chewing, the pancake dissolving in her mouth. Mary Kate sounded so matter-of-fact as she made the leap from spending the day with Cole to living with him. Didn't she know what a momentous thing she was talking about? Jane swallowed before answering carefully. "Until the house sells, you'll have ample opportunity to visit with your father and Stephanie. Once we move to Melbourne we can still visit from time to time. Maybe they'll come and see us, too."

Mary Kate stacked two pieces of cut pancakes onto her fork. "Couldn't we, like, all live together somewhere?"

"I'm sorry, that's not possible." Jane abruptly rose to check the pancakes in the frying pan. She flipped them and returned to her seat. "Cole and I have our own lives. I don't want to live in Red Hill and he doesn't want to live in Melbourne. We could live in the middle but then no one would be happy. Not that we would live anywhere *together*."

"But you loved him…"

"That was a long time ago," Jane said. "Cole and I aren't teenagers anymore." A sudden thought occurred to her. "Whatever you do, don't talk to your father about what I felt once upon a time. Whether it was real love or puppy love, I don't feel that now."

"Oh, okay," Mary Kate said, instantly subdued.

Jane studied her daughter as she intently wiped up syrup with a piece of pancake on her fork. "You haven't already said something to him, have you?"

Mary Kate shook her head.

"That's a relief."

The phone rang. Jane picked up then handed over the receiver. "Cole wants to talk to you."

The shy, eager smile on Mary Kate's face as she said hello into the phone to her father made Jane turn away, hugging herself. As painful as it was, she had to accept that her daughter was no longer solely hers. But then, she never had been.

"THANKS," Mary Kate said, accepting a soft drink from Cole. With her other hand she clutched the ferry railing while the wind whipped her hair around her face.

Sorrento, with its historic limestone buildings, was receding and Queenscliff, where Cole was taking her for lunch, was still half an hour away on the other side of the bay. In the past weeks she'd only been with him in the company of Stephanie. Now, on her own, it was easier to look at the waves than meet Cole's gaze.

"Keep your eye out for dolphins." He, too, seemed to prefer scanning the horizon as he sipped steaming coffee.

"Okay…" She realized she didn't know what to call him. Until now she hadn't been in a situation where she had to call him anything. She wanted to say *Dad* but felt self-conscious. Avoiding a decision, she pointed to a dark blip in the water to the right of the boat. "Is that one?"

Cole shielded his eyes from the sun glinting off the waves. "No, that's a clump of kelp. When you see a dolphin, you'll know. They travel in pods of five to ten animals."

Mary Kate breathed in the salty air and then lifted her sun-warmed cheeks to the cooling ocean spray. Cole talked about the bay, trying to make her feel at ease. There was so much she wanted to say, so many things she wanted to ask, but she felt tongue-tied and shy. She had to say *something*. "What's Stephanie doing today?"

"She's shopping with her mother," Cole said. "School is coming up in a few weeks and she needs new shoes."

"Mom says I'll have to wear a school uniform," Mary Kate said, screwing up her face.

"It's not so bad. A gingham dress is standard for the girls and shorts and a polo shirt for the boys. Every school has different colors. Stephanie's uniform is white and navy." He glanced in her direction. "Those colors would look good on you."

Mary Kate felt her cheeks warm. "I don't know where I'll be going to school yet. It depends on whether Mom buys the apartment. And that depends on selling the farm." She chipped at the thick enamel paint on the railing, wondering if she should say she'd like to stay in Red Hill. Or would that be disloyal to Mom?

"Did your mother tell you that I grew up on that farm?"

Mary Kate flashed him a glance. She only caught his profile, but something in the somber line of his mouth gave her the impression of sadness. "Why did you move away?"

"My father sold it to pay some debts."

"Why don't you buy it back?"

"It's not that simple."

"That's what grown-ups always say when they don't want to tell you the real reason."

Cole chuckled and said lightly, "You're a smart girl. Must take after your old man."

Her cheeks heated with pleasure and embarrassment. "Yeah, I guess."

"What are your favorite subjects at school?"

"Math and P.E."

"No kidding? Mine, too. I play Australian rules football and squash, a bit of cricket… anything really, when I have time."

Mary Kate responded eagerly, turning to talk directly to him. "I was pitcher on the school softball team in California. And I like soccer, too. And basketball."

"Stephanie plays netball. It's somewhat similar to basketball. Maybe you could go out for the same team—" Cole broke off. "If, that is, you were going to the same school. When footy season starts again, I'll take you to a game, if you like."

"Thanks, I would."

"What else do you like to do besides shopping and riding horses?"

"Well…" Mary Kate said, her mind racing. "I like Sudoku. When we get the newspaper, Mom does the crossword and I do the Sudoku."

"*I* like Sudoku. Usually at work, in between clients." Cole lowered his voice to a conspiratorial whisper. "Don't tell Millie, though, or she'll find something else for me to do."

Mary Kate giggled. She looked over the waves. A freighter was steaming past, on its way to Melbourne, a distant clump of tall buildings off to their right. "Mom's smart, too."

"I know she is."

Mary Kate's ears perked up. He sounded as if he admired her mom. She couldn't work out whether her mom and Cole liked each other now or not. They seemed to argue a lot. Although she'd noticed that often her mom checked out Cole when she thought he wasn't looking. And vice versa. Jane had *said* there was no chance of her and Cole getting back together, but…

"Did you—" She broke off.

"What?" Cole regarded her kindly. "Go on, you can ask me anything."

"Did you love my mother? Back then, I mean?"

Cole's gaze jerked back to the water. Mary Kate wished she hadn't asked. But after what seemed like ages, he said softly, "Yeah, I loved her."

"What about now?" Mary Kate ventured.

"Now?" He straightened and tossed back the rest of his coffee. "It's too late for us."

His voice had hardened to match the severe lines of his mouth. But he hadn't said no…

Cole's foam cup emitted a faint squeak as he turned it around in his long fingers. "Do you wish you had a different father?"

Mary Kate was so startled by the question her hand jumped and cola foamed over her fingers. "No! You're okay. Better than okay." She smiled up at him shyly. "You're *great*."

His wide smile warmed her insides as he handed her a tissue. While she was still wiping the sticky sweetness off, Cole set their drinks on the deck and wrapped her in a bear hug. Mary Kate wriggled her arms out from between them and hugged him back. For a moment they stood entwined and it was just perfect.

Then Cole turned her toward the ocean where a trio of sleek black dolphins arced out of the waves. "Look! There they are."

Sunlight gleamed off the animals' smooth curves and the salt spray sparkled on a falling curtain of water. Mary Kate felt the gentle pressure of her father's arm around her shoulders, supporting her. Tears welled in her eyes. "Awesome."

"MOM!" MARY KATE RAN ahead of Cole into the farmhouse. "Where are you? I'm home."

Cole followed, smoothing down his windblown hair. The smell of fresh paint was overpowering. In the lounge room, the furniture had been pushed away from the walls and draped in old sheets. Jane, wearing very short cutoffs and a skinny T-shirt, was halfway up a stepladder, spreading creamy paint over the dingy green walls with a roller. When she stretched forward, he could see a hint of her bottom through the fringe of white threads.

"Hi, honey. Did you have a good day?" Without looking around, Jane continued to roll on paint. "I'll be with you as soon as I finish this…last…little…patch."

"I'm going to change. We called Stephanie on the way back. She'll be here soon." Mary Kate's last words were almost drowned out by her footsteps thumping up the stairs.

Cole cleared his throat. Jane twisted around. She let go of her grip on the ladder to tug down her shorts and almost fell off. "I didn't know you were here. I assumed you would just drop her off."

"I wanted to talk to you." Cole walked over and took the roller from her, laying it in the paint tray. He glanced around at the cream-colored walls, gleaming with fresh paint. "If you fix the place up you may not want to leave."

"I'm burying the past, not preparing for the future." She climbed down and stepped back to survey her handiwork. "Although I must admit, something about fresh paint inspires optimism. This room looks completely different, doesn't it?"

"It's great." Specks of cream paint dotted her arms and coffee-colored T-shirt. With the afternoon sunlight gilding her blond hair, she looked about twenty. His fingers itched to wipe away the splotch on one flushed cheek. "You've got paint on you…" His voice came out unexpectedly husky.

Jane's gaze met his, brief and burning. Her cheeks turned a deeper shade of pink as she glanced away, wiping at her skin with the back of her hand. "How did it go?"

"We saw dolphins," he said, taking a step back. "We bonded over Sudoku."

She glanced around sharply. "I can't do Sudoku."

"Luckily, it's not an essential life skill," he said mildly. "We have the same laugh. We both like horror flicks."

"Don't let it go to your head." Jane

picked up the tray and roller and started for the door to the kitchen.

Cole started after her, discovered he'd stepped in paint and had to stop and wipe his shoe on a rag. When he caught up, she was at the laundry-room sink, running water into the tray. "Why are you so insecure about my relationship with Mary Kate?"

"I'm not." Moodily, she pushed the roller around, not looking at him.

"She's my daughter. I have a right to spend time with her." He spoke calmly, trying to be patient. But inside, a familiar resentment was building. Jane had had Mary Kate for nearly twelve years. Did she really begrudge him a single day with her? "If we enjoy each other's company that's a *good* thing."

Jane snapped off the running tap. Facing him, she jabbed a paint-stained finger at his chest. "Go ahead and do your little Sudoku puzzles but don't you dare think for one moment that she's going to live with you."

"As a matter of fact, I *am* thinking that," he said. "Why shouldn't she live with me for a while? She could go to school here in Red Hill with Stephanie. I want to buy her a horse of her own to ride."

Jane spun around, her face pale. "She doesn't know how to look after a horse. Where would she keep it? You only have two box stalls at your place."

She was ignoring his wish for Mary Kate to live with him and focusing on the horse, throwing any objection she could think of. Cole responded without thinking. "Here on the farm."

"Are you nuts? I'm selling Cockatoo Ridge. *If* you ever find me a buyer, that is."

"I *have* found a buyer," he snapped. And immediately regretted speaking. He hadn't intended saying anything until he'd tied down the financing.

She blinked. "Really? Who?"

Bloody hell. "*I* want to buy the farm."

Surprise widened Jane's eyes. Without a word, she turned back to the sink and finished rinsing the roller, using her nails to push the cream out of the pink fuzz.

"Well?" he demanded. "Aren't you

happy? This is good news for you. Now you can buy your apartment."

She turned off the tap and shook the roller then propped it inside the sink. "Can you afford it?"

Cole bristled. "That's not your concern."

"Anything that affects my daughter's welfare is my concern." She waited a beat. "Isn't there a conflict of interest here? As the agent you should be trying to get me the best price. As the buyer you'll naturally want to pay as little as possible."

"I admit, it's tricky." Cole scratched his head. "I'll waive my commission. You can take that amount off the top. And if I can sell the Rasmussen estate—and at the moment that's a pretty big if—then the deal will be viable."

"What's the Rasmussen estate?"

"A multimillion-dollar property between Red Hill and Western Port Bay. Fifty hectares, ten-bedroom house, stables, sheds, swimming pool, et cetera, et cetera. Immaculate condition, top-quality materials."

"There can't be a big market for such an exclusive property," Jane said skeptically. "Have you got any potential buyers lined up?"

"I've got a few," Cole bluffed. Then he had a thought. "This actor friend of yours, Rafe Baldwyn, maybe he's interested in a country property. A retreat for when Hollywood gets too much."

"Maybe," Jane said doubtfully.

"Could you introduce me to him?"

"He's busy doing interviews and promoting the film, but I'll see what I can do." Jane wrapped her arms around her waist. "So is this official? Are you making me an offer on the farm?"

Cole swallowed. It was too soon but he couldn't back down now. He wanted Cockatoo Ridge almost as much as he wanted Mary Kate, almost as much as he wanted… "Nine hundred thousand."

"I'm asking the full market price, remember? I'm having a lot of work done on the house."

"Nine-fifty is my best offer. And as I said, I'll waive my commission."

Jane's lips pressed together as her jaw tightened. Cole got the distinct impression that for some reason she didn't want to sell to him.

"You're not likely to get a better offer," he told her.

There was a long pause. "Okay, then."

Cole felt no release of tension as he held out a hand to stiffly shake on the deal. "Get me the meeting with Baldwyn."

Somehow, he would do the rest.

CHAPTER SEVEN

MARY KATE PACED the veranda, watching for Stephanie and Magoo. Only a few hours ago her mom and dad had both admitted to having been in love with each other. Now they were fighting. Who knew what was going to happen next? Grown-ups were so *random*.

"Hi," Stephanie called, riding up the hill on Magoo. She led a saddled and bridled Cherry. Tossing Cherry's reins to Mary Kate, she said, "Let's ride down by the creek."

"Okay." Mary Kate stuck her foot in the stirrup and swung up. Cherry stepped forward but Mary Kate clung to the pommel and got her leg over the saddle. She settled her feet firmly in the stirrups and wiggled her butt to a comfortable position, checking that the reins were even and had the right amount of tension. She was aware of Stephanie watching and was pleased when her sister smiled and headed off. She felt like an old hand already.

They cut diagonally across and down the hill and were soon walking single file beside a dry creek bed that twisted and turned between shady gum trees. Stephanie rode ahead and Mary Kate, on Cherry, plodded a few paces behind.

"The creek dries up in summer but there's a water hole up ahead," Stephanie said. "We'll stop there."

"Did you know this creek is where my mom and our dad met?" Mary Kate said. "He found a baby possum and they took care of it together."

"Cool. What did you and Dad do in Queenscliff?"

"We ate fish and chips on the beach. We saw dolphins on the ferry over *and* on the way back." Mary Kate transferred the reins to one hand and smoothed out a tangle in Cherry's long black mane. "Did you find some shoes?"

"Yes, for school. Bor-ing! I wanted to

go to Melbourne to that boutique you were telling me about, but Mum wouldn't drive that far."

"We're going to the city sometime this week. You can come with us."

"That would be great. Next week, I'm starting classes to get my bronze medallion in swimming. Do you want to do it, too?"

"I'll have to ask my mom. I don't know how long we're staying."

Stephanie pulled Magoo to a halt beside a small dark pool bordered by ferns and fallen logs. She slid off, looped the reins loosely around her horse's neck and let him go. Magoo nibbled at the dry grass.

Mary Kate did the same with Cherry. Then she lay on her stomach on the bank next to Stephanie and plucked a stalk of grass to chew. An idea had been brewing and she wanted Stephanie's opinion. "Does Cole have a girlfriend?"

"He went out with a lady in Flinders for a while but that fizzled out." Stephanie made a face. "I was glad. She called me 'kitten' and petted me on the head."

"I wish Cole and my mother had never

split in the first place." Then Mary Kate realized what she'd said. "Sorry. That wouldn't have been so great for *your* mom."

Stephanie sat up and hugged her knees to her chest. "I wish *my* mum and dad had never split up. But I guess they weren't happy. Mum said they were pressured into getting married by their families. They must have loved each other at one point if I'm around."

"I'm sure they did," Mary Kate said. "What's your stepfather like?"

"Fergus? He's really nice. Mum's crazy about him. I'm glad about that. Everybody's friends now, so that makes it easier."

Stephanie frowned and tossed a pebble in the water. "I worry about Dad, though. He doesn't have anyone special. He works all the time. And Uncle Joey is always getting into trouble and Dad has to bail him out."

"Joey must be my half uncle, if there's such a thing," Mary Kate mused. "My wicked uncle Joey."

Stephanie giggled. "He's pretty funny, really."

Mary Kate chewed furiously on her blade of grass. "Mom doesn't have a boyfriend. But I've been thinking. There's no reason she and Cole can't get together again."

"You mean, get married?"

"Why not?" Mary Kate asked. "They both admitted to me they used to be in love. It's not like either of them has met anyone better in all these years. Deep down, they're probably pining for each other."

"If it would make Dad happy, I'm all for it. I like your mum. She's got a great laugh."

Mary Kate fell silent, contemplating the possibilities. "If they got married it would be good for us. We'd *really* be sisters."

Stephanie's face lit. Then she subsided almost instantly. "They've been apart a long time. Dad says he's not interested in getting married."

"That's what Mom says. But I noticed she put perfume on before she came to pick me up at your place last week. She hardly ever wears perfume."

Stephanie nodded, conceding this was

an important point. "Dad ironed his polo shirt. He *never* irons unless it's for work or he's going out on a date."

"I bet they *do* like each other, even if they don't always act like it," Mary Kate said. "They just can't see it yet. We'll have to help them."

"We'll throw them together," Stephanie suggested.

"Yes!" Mary Kate agreed excitedly. "I'll tell Mom I want to spend time with Cole but I don't want *her* to feel left out so she has to come along, too. You, too, because I don't want to hog him or anything."

"But how can they fall in love if we're there?" Stephanie argued. "It would be better if they were alone."

"True." Mary Kate thought a moment. "I know! They could go on a romantic horseback ride on the beach." She squared her fingers and thumbs the way a movie director framed a shot. "Afternoon, white sand, blue sky. Mom riding bareback, her hair flowing, her dress fluttering. Cole, looking like a pirate, galloping after her."

"A pirate? You mean with an eye patch?"

"Maybe not the patch," Mary Kate conceded. "I was thinking about one of those billowy white shirts with the ruffles down the front."

"Dad wouldn't be caught dead in something like that," Stephanie said. "He'd look fine in his green shirt, the one that matches his eyes."

"They'll need champagne," Mary Kate said.

"Dad's got heaps of bottles in his wine shed."

"I'll put together a picnic. But it has to be a surprise or they won't agree to go together."

"I'll ask Dad to ride with me down to the beach," Stephanie said. "You get your mum to drive down—"

"We'll just happen to run into each other—"

"And I'll say I'd rather go swimming with you—"

"They'll ride together just like the good old days," Mary Kate finished. "Before long, Mom and Dad will be whispering sweet nothings."

"OUCH! I THINK I just broke my pelvis," Jane cried as she landed on the horse's withers after Cole gave her a leg up onto Cherry. "Explain to me again why we aren't using saddles."

"Stephanie wanted to ride in the surf, and salt stains the leather." Cole handed Jane the reins. "You don't have to do this, you know."

"Don't I?" Jane grumbled. "Stephanie practically threw the reins at me before she ran into the water with Mary Kate for a swim. I shouldn't even be here today. I have a million phone calls to make for the premiere."

"I'm not happy about the way this has turned out, either." Cole grabbed a handful of mane, planted a hand on Magoo's rump and swung onto the gelding's back. "You realize we're being set up, don't you?"

"You think?" Jane replied dryly. "Mary Kate wanted me to wear my good silk blouse, never mind that it would get ruined."

"Stephanie tried to get me to wear her art smock in the hopes I would resemble Captain Jack Sparrow. I pointed out that without a cutlass I'd look more like an oversize kindergarten kid about to do finger painting."

Cole led the way to the water's edge where the sand was hard packed. "By the way, have you spoken to Rafe Baldwyn about the Rasmussen estate?"

"Not yet. I called this morning but he wasn't answering his phone." Jane walked Cherry into the shallow water where white foam surged around the horse's fetlocks. Farther down the beach near the rocky point, a surf fisherman cast his line into the blue water. She gave herself up to the gentle rhythm of Cherry's swaying walk. Maybe taking a break from work wasn't such a bad thing.

Cole broke into her thoughts. "Are you game for a canter?"

"You're on." Without further notice, Jane leaned over Cherry's neck and dug her heels in. The horse lunged forward, her hind hooves churning up the sand as she sped off down the beach.

Magoo, hating to be left behind, began to gallop. The Arab gelding was faster than

the bay mare and quickly caught up to
Cherry, his arched neck stretched forward
and his silver mane streaming back. As
they shot past, Jane urged her horse on. For
a few seconds they ran neck and neck. Jane
laughed, exhilarated and breathless. Then
Cole pulled out in front again and galloped
on ahead.

As they neared the part of the beach
where swimmers and sunbathers congre-
gated, Cole sat back, reining Magoo into a
canter. Sweat lathered the horses' necks and
chests and their nostrils blew wide. They
slowed to a trot then a walk, then turned and
started back the way they'd come.

Jane came alongside Cole. "I haven't
ridden like that in years."

"I don't do it often enough," Cole
admitted.

They continued toward the picnic sight.
The girls had come out of the water and
were drying themselves off with brightly
colored beach towels.

"Wait till you see what they brought,"
Jane chuckled. "Mary Kate insisted on
packing it herself but I had a peek. Smoked

oysters, chocolate spread and canned asparagus."

"Am I supposed to spot the odd one out? Is it chocolate?"

"They're all aphrodisiacs."

"Good Lord."

"Kids are so cute, aren't they?"

"Stephanie raided my wine fridge when she thought I wasn't looking and smuggled a bottle over to your house," Cole said. "I hope she chose a good vintage."

"Does she know a good vintage from a bad one?"

"She'd better not."

Jane exchanged a smile with him over their daughters' antics and they lapsed into a companionable silence. After a moment she glanced over at Cole. His dark hair had been tousled by the breeze, and with an open-neck shirt instead of that damn tie, he looked incredibly sexy—

What was she thinking? She'd been seduced by the beautiful day, the carefree ride along the beach. She'd do well to remember exactly why she couldn't let Cole get under her skin. The day she'd left

Red Hill was etched permanently on her heart, even though she tried to think of that painful time as little as possible.

She'd been devastated when Cole had asked Leslie to marry him after he'd found out she was pregnant. But Jane had believed his regret to be sincere when he'd told her they couldn't see each other anymore. He'd seemed desperately sorry when later she'd learned *she* was pregnant, too. He'd offered to support her and the baby even though that was clearly beyond his capabilities, no matter how hardworking and determined he was. She'd felt sorry for him, he was torn in so many different directions.

But when she'd said goodbye to him before leaving for the airport, he'd hit her with a blow she'd never recovered from. He'd told her straight out, *I don't love you.* He couldn't have been more blunt and cruel.

"I think it's only fair to warn you that they're wasting their time," Jane said abruptly.

"I beg your pardon?" Cole pressed the reins against Magoo's neck, turning the horse and coming closer so he could hear over the waves and the gulls.

Jane swallowed. Closer wasn't a good idea. His hands, his thighs, the movement of his body in rhythm with the horse, all combined to make her achingly conscious of what they'd had together. And what she'd lost. There had been a few other men but no one had captured her, body and soul, the way Cole had. It had taken her a long time to get over him. Now that she had, she wasn't going to fall for him again.

"I said, the girls are barking up the wrong tree if they think you and I are going to…" She paused, her throat suddenly dry at the intense look in his eyes.

"What?" he asked.

"You know, fall in love."

"*Love.*" He snorted. "The older I get, the harder it is to find. I doubt it'll pop up in a tin of asparagus."

Right. That pretty much summed up her feelings, too.

By the time they returned to the grassy picnic site, Mary Kate and Stephanie had spread the blanket. Cole filled a bucket with fresh water, and Magoo thrust his nose in and drank thirstily. When he'd finished, Cherry drank her fill.

Cole was leading the horses over to a shady tree to tether them when Stephanie took the reins out of his hands. "Our turn."

"The horses need a rest," Cole objected.

"Mary Kate has never ridden bareback," Jane added.

"We won't go faster than a walk," Stephanie said. "The worst that could happen is that Mary Kate might slide off into soft sand." Casually, she added, "You two can go ahead and start eating."

Before Jane or Cole could call them back, Stephanie gave Mary Kate a leg up onto Cherry and swung herself onto Magoo's back. Jane glanced at Cole and shrugged. The girls' machinations would have no effect.

Cole poured them glasses of warm champagne while she spread Nutella over crackers. "To daughters," he said, raising his glass.

"And fine dining," she added, clinking. "They're not going to be successful."

His cool detachment showed Jane just how true that statement was—for him.

Keeping her gaze empty of emotion, she replied, "Absolutely not."

COLE STUDIED the bank statements for the Red Hill Real Estate trust account. A sick feeling carved a hole in his stomach. Something was dreadfully wrong. Twice during the past month, cash had been taken out of the account and then returned within a few weeks. Five hundred here, two hundred there…

"Joey!" Cole bellowed, ignoring the office intercom. "Get in my office, now!"

Too furious to sit still, Cole snatched up the bank statements and met Joey coming out of his office. Cole pushed him back inside and shut the door. He threw the statements onto Joey's desk amid a mess of sandwich wrappers, listings and scribbled memos. "Have you been embezzling from the company account?"

Joey cringed. "Embezzling is such a nasty word. Borrowing would be more accurate. If you'll note, both times I paid the money back well before it was needed." He smiled hopefully. "No harm done?"

"No harm?" Cole stabbed at a line on the statement. "You went into the business account and transferred money to your own. That's a crime."

"I didn't want to bother you for another loan. Anyway, you weren't here to ask when I needed it. I don't know why you're so upset. I gave the money back."

Joey's excuses and casual attitude only made Cole madder. Slapping his hands onto the desk, he leaned across, getting right in Joey's face. "This is my business. It's not just me who depends on Red Hill Real Estate. There's you and Millie, not to mention Stephanie and sometimes Mum. Now Mary Kate. What you did was *illegal.* You can't get away with it just because you're my little brother."

"Chill out, mate," Joey said, rearing back in alarm. "It's not the end of the world."

"No, but it's the end of your employment here." He righted the pencil holder he'd knocked over with his fist. "You're fired!"

Joey sat up straight, finally realizing Cole was seriously upset. "You don't mean that."

"Too bloody right I do." Cole pointed to the exit. "Go. And don't come back."

"I DON'T KNOW what you mean." Mary Kate was studiously innocent as she dipped her brush in paint and began covering the grayish pink inside the fridge alcove with fresh cream-colored paint.

"Oh, really?" Jane said. "That romantic picnic on the beach wasn't designed to try to bring Cole and me together?"

The old stove had been ripped out and taken to the tip. The new stove was waiting in the garage for the painting to be completed before William Lasky came back to install it. These days he was a big strapping guy with perfectly straight teeth.

Mary Kate turned to face Jane, her brush dripping on the spread newspapers. "Well, why not? It's not like you've got another man in your life."

"Gee, thanks."

"I mean it," Mary Kate persisted. "He's cool. Plus, he's my father."

Jane carefully placed her roller in the

tray and wiped her hands on a rag. "I understand how it would seem to make sense for us to marry. You'd have a whole family, a mother, father and a half sister."

Just for a moment, it made sense to *her,* too. Rosy images of the four of them living in the renovated farmhouse rolled through her mind like a family movie. Until she remembered this was real life, not fiction.

"Except that I don't love him. And he doesn't love me."

"Do you *like* him?" Mary Kate persisted.

"I am trying to get along with him because he's your father. And because it's the mature thing to do. However, that's where I draw the line. I don't *love* him," she said firmly. "I'm not going to date him. We will not turn into the Brady Bunch."

"Who?"

"Never mind. Just don't do any more matchmaking, because it isn't going to work."

"Okay," Mary Kate said too easily.

"Okay?" Jane persisted, not satisfied.

"Okay," Mary Kate said, aggrieved.

Jane was quiet a few minutes. Maybe Mary Kate was looking for some sort of reassurance. "I'm glad that you're getting along so well with Cole. Even though I'm not interested in renewing my relationship with him, I'm fine with *you* having a relationship. As long as…"

"As long as I don't go live with him?"

Jane turned back to her painting. She'd be a hypocrite if she denied she'd be devastated if Mary Kate chose to live with her father.

"Mom?" Mary Kate said tentatively.

"I want to finish this today. Can we get back to work, please?"

Mary Kate touched Jane's shoulder. "It's not going to be a problem. I wouldn't go if you didn't want me to."

Jane felt tears squeeze through her eyelashes. "You and Stephanie can stay overnight…often. Would that be enough?"

"Sure. That'd be fine." Mary Kate moved away and plugged her MP3 earphones in to the sound of tinny music.

Jane let her breath go. To be flayed by doubts. Would it be fine with *Cole?* Was it *really* fine with Mary Kate? Or did her daughter recognize that *Jane* was the one who needed reassurance?

They finished the first coat and took a break. While Jane made sandwiches, Mary Kate ran upstairs to call Stephanie.

"She gave me a lecture about not doing any more matchmaking," Mary Kate said to Stephanie over the phone as she lay on her back with her head toward the end of the bed.

"Dad did the same," Stephanie complained. "What are we going to do?"

"We'll have to be less obvious. Get them to go somewhere more glamorous. Someplace they won't get sand in their teeth." She studied the old movie posters curling away from the wall at the corners. And shot upright on the bed. "Of course! The movie premiere. Mom's going to need a date. Cole would be perfect. We just need to trick her into asking him. He's such a gentleman he'd never refuse."

"A premiere!" squealed Stephanie. "Oh my God. I'm hyperventilating. Is it red carpet and everything?"

"Naturally. Does Cole own a tux?"

"The one he wore at his wedding is

hanging in the closet. I'll check it for moth holes."

"Excellent. But Mom will have to have a new dress." Mary Kate laughed, hugging herself. "Ooh, I feel a shopping expedition coming on."

CHAPTER EIGHT

"YOU CAN'T BUY a dress for the premiere from a chain store," Mary Kate informed her mother, tugging on her hand to lead her out of the multistory mall at Melbourne Central. "I know this cool street with heaps of boutiques."

Stephanie trailed behind, awed by more shops than she'd seen in her whole life. She clutched bags containing pretty new tops and skirts and a pair of sandals that had been on sale.

"What would you know about where to shop in Melbourne?" Jane asked, bemused at her daughter's insistence on haute couture. Mary Kate had always been interested in clothes but usually she left Jane to pick out her own.

"I looked it up on the Internet." She

paused at the corner before striding down a narrow brick-paved lane. Signs hanging from wrought-iron frames dotted both sides of the lane, enticing shoppers into tiny showrooms where stylish women presided over a select display of gorgeous gowns by local and overseas designers. "Who are you taking, by the way?"

"I'm not even sure I'm going," Jane protested.

"You have tickets, don't you?"

"I get two passes, but that doesn't mean I have to use them…" She trailed off as her gaze lit on a shimmering ivory creation in the window. It was embroidered with gold thread and decorated with hundreds of tiny gold beads in an intricate design that followed the flowing lines of the figure-hugging shape, ending in just a hint of a train. "Oh, my!"

"Wow!" Stephanie echoed, her mouth dropping open.

"It's you," Mary Kate declared and marched inside. She went straight up to the long-nosed woman with the jet-black bob behind the high marble desk. "My mother would like to try on the dress in the window."

"Certainly, miss," the salesclerk replied without a trace of mockery. She looked Jane up and down. "Size eight?"

"Yes, but I have no intention of purchasing a dress today," Jane said firmly. "Don't get too comfortable," she added to Stephanie, who had collapsed on a settee surrounded by her bags and parcels.

"Just try it on, Mom. *Please.*" Mary Kate clasped both hands beneath beseeching eyes.

"For goodness' sake." Jane laughed, then hushed as the saleswoman floated the dress past her on the way to the fitting room. A sudden attack of fashion lust swept over her. It had been ages since she'd had anything new and the dress *was* spectacular. "I suppose it wouldn't hurt to try it on."

As Jane slipped inside the fitting room, she heard Mary Kate ask, "Do you have a pair of shoes to match?"

Jane slipped the dress over her head just as a pair of ivory satin heels were pushed under the door. She zipped up and turned to look at herself in the mirror. The strapless dress fit her perfectly. She stepped into the shoes and opened the door to a chorus of oohs and aahs from Mary Kate and Stephanie.

Even the saleswoman's crimson lips pursed in surprised admiration as Jane made her way to the trio of folding mirrors on a dais. "It might have been made for you."

Jane swirled to and fro, amazed at her reflection, and delighted with how fabulous the well-cut dress made her feel. Even the shoes were perfect.

"You look like a princess," Stephanie breathed.

"She'll take it," Mary Kate declared.

Jane stopped swirling to face the trio. "I can't buy this dress."

"Why not?" Mary Kate wanted to know.

"Because…well…" Offhand, she couldn't think of a compelling reason. Then she caught sight of a tiny price tag dangling discreetly under her left armpit. The dollar amount made her gasp. "*That's* why not."

"I'll go without a winter coat this year," Mary Kate offered.

"Try the next decade."

"You *have* to have that dress."

Stephanie nodded. "You do, really."

Jane glanced back to the mirror and slid her hands over her hips, admitting the truth to herself. She coveted the dress. It made her feel feminine and beautiful. But it was a waste since she knew from experience that gala events were no fun on her own.

Mary Kate came closer and spoke in a low voice. "What's stopping you, Mom?"

Jane met her daughter's gaze, a little disconcerted by how grown-up Mary Kate sounded. "I have no one to go with."

"You could ask Cole."

"So that's where all this has been leading. Did I not make myself clear, Mary Kate? You girls are not manipulating me and Cole into another date." Jane stepped off the dais and swished back to the fitting room, shutting the door behind her.

Outside she could hear Stephanie and Mary Kate's indistinct voices, snatches floating to her… Cole…the premiere. She tuned them out. Asking Cole to the premiere was out of the question. She didn't want to. And he probably wouldn't come anyway.

Jane caught sight of herself again in the mirror. She felt a twinge at the swift passage of time. How long had it been since she'd gotten dressed up and gone out on the town? Her fingers traced the sleek lines. She was thirty. How long before she was no longer young and attractive enough to wear a dress like this?

She twisted in front of the mirror, wondering what Cole would think of her appearance. Would he be tempted to sweep his hand over her bare back, to glide his fingers along the satiny smoothness of her hips, to press a kiss in the pillowy softness where her breasts met above the bodice?

Her phone rang. Jane clicked it on and before she could even say hello, Rafe's gravelly voice filled her ear. "It's all your fault. Now you've got to save me."

"Save you from what?" Jane asked, reaching around her back to unzip.

"Mia." He lowered his voice. "She's insisting we attend the premiere as a couple. I know I have to pretend to like her in

public, but *at a distance.* Spending the whole evening with that woman clinging to my arm would send me to the loony bin."

Jane stepped out of the dress and tucked the phone on her shoulder so she could reach for the hanger. "What do you want *me* to do?"

"Be my date."

"I haven't even decided if I'm going."

"You are now. I'm calling in favors, so don't try to get out of it," Rafe warned. "I've already told her it's arranged."

"Okay, I'll be your date," Jane said. "Before you hang up, I've been meaning to tell you about a fantastic property for sale in Red Hill. Mary Kate's father is a real estate agent and he's handling it. Apparently it's gorgeous. You came from the country. I thought you might want to get back to your roots and all that. Are you interested?"

"I am, as a matter of fact," Rafe began when there was a scuffling sound and Mia came on the line.

"*You're* going with Rafe?" the actress

shrilled. "What about *me?* Now I have no one to go with."

"What about—" Jane began then broke off, remembering Mia's scandalous breakup from her most recent boyfriend. "Well, you must know lots of eligible men."

"Everyone I know is in L.A.! What are you going to do about this?"

"Me?" Jane asked, incredulous.

"Rafe was going to go with me until you crooked your little finger," Mia said petulantly. "The least you can do is find me an escort."

Jane groaned. This was *so* not in her job description. But then ninety percent of the things she did weren't.

"Mom?" Mary Kate was at the door. "Are you okay in there?"

"I'll be out in a minute," she said, covering the phone with her hand. Then she went back to Mia. "I'll see what I can do."

"All right. But no jerks and no married men."

"Yes, yes. Goodbye." Jane started to put her own clothes back on.

"Mom?"

"I'm buying the dress."

"Are you going to the premiere?"

"Yes," Jane said, resigned.

"Hooray," Mary Kate and Stephanie cheered together.

With the most dazzling frock she'd ever owned carefully wrapped in tissue paper and tucked inside a glossy shopping bag, Jane took the girls to lunch at a hole-in-the-wall pizzeria down another laneway. Stephanie commented on the minimalist toppings, and Mary Kate, the authority on everything metropolitan, explained that was because it was authentic Italian. Jane had to smile, listening to them argue and laugh. She had to admit, Mary Kate was a lot happier about the move to Australia since she'd met Stephanie. And the way Stephanie's eyes shone suggested she was equally thrilled with her new sister and best friend.

"Are you girls done?" Jane rose and brushed crumbs from her fingers. "I have an appointment with the real estate agent at the apartment. I want one more look and then I'm going to make an offer."

Mary Kate glanced at Stephanie in alarm then turned to her mother. "I didn't know you were doing that today."

"It won't take long," Jane assured her. "I thought you'd like to show Stephanie where you'll be living."

Any hopes Mary Kate had that her mom had forgotten about buying the apartment were dashed. Mary Kate was silent as they walked back to the parking lot and picked up the car for the short trip to Docklands.

At the massive sports arena, Jane turned left toward the waterfront where high-rise apartment buildings clustered around restaurants, shops, galleries and public space. She parked outside the apartment building and they got out of the car. Gusts of wind whipped across the vast expanse of barren concrete that surrounded the complex.

Stephanie looked around, bewildered. "Where are the trees?"

"There's one. It even comes with its own livestock." Mary Kate pointed to a lone tree with a life-size papier-mâché cow perched upside down in the spindly branches.

"Okay, that's just weird," Stephanie commented.

"Docklands is still new. There'll be more trees and shrubs planted in good time," Jane assured them. "Let's go inside."

Jason, the real estate agent, was about Uncle Joey's age but slicker. He let them into the empty apartment. Mary Kate wrinkled her nose at a faint chemical smell and traced it to the plush champagne-colored carpet that sank beneath her feet.

Jane glided through the apartment, murmuring words like *magnificent* and *fabulous* as she spun from the floor-to-ceiling windows overlooking the harbor, to the sunken fireplace, to the kitchen cleverly disguised as part of the dining room. The fridge, stove and sink were hidden in a walk-in pantry. Compared to the huge country kitchen at the farmhouse it was prettier, but it wasn't as homey.

Mary Kate touched her mom's sleeve. "It's kind of small, isn't it?"

"That doesn't matter. We'll probably eat out a lot. There are so many restaurants and convenience stores nearby." Jane peered into her face. "Honey, what's wrong? You loved the apartment the first time we saw it."

Mary Kate chewed her lip. "I'll be so far away from Red Hill. From Cole and Stephanie. And my horse."

Jane pressed her lips together. "You don't have a horse yet. And we are not staying in Red Hill. A couple of weeks ago you wanted to move into this apartment as much as I do."

"I can change my mind, can't I?"

"No, actually, you can't. Why don't you show Stephanie the second bedroom. You girls can plan a sleepover for after we move in."

"Come on, Stephanie." Mary Kate led her into a bland white box with a view of the city through miniblinds. "This is it."

Stephanie glanced around. "It's very clean."

And that was about all that could be said about it. Mary Kate bit her lip, frowning. There was no way she was going to live here, so far from her sister and her father.

There had to be some means of stopping her mom from buying the place.

Mary Kate left Stephanie to look through the rest of the apartment and went back out to the lounge room.

"I'd like to make an offer," Jane was saying to Jason. "Six-fifty."

"The asking price is seven twenty-five," Jason reminded her. "We had a lot of interest at the open house on the weekend. But I'll convey your offer to the vendor and let you know. If he's agreeable we'll need a deposit immediately."

Mary Kate sidled forward. "What happens if someone else says they'll pay more than my mom?"

Jason smiled as if she were a particularly bright six-year-old. "Until the contract note is signed, the vendor may accept other bids. Of course, your mother would be given the opportunity to increase her amount."

"So, if another offer was made, you'd have to take it to the vendor, then come back to my mom then go back to the other person then back to the vendor—" Mary

Kate stopped, having run out of breath. "That would take a while."

"It could," Jason agreed. "Especially if both parties really want the property and got into a bidding war."

All the way home in the car, Jane tapped her fingers on the steering wheel and fretted. "I should have started with a higher offer."

"You can always go up," Stephanie remarked from the backseat. "That's what my dad always advises people."

"Your father knows what he's talking about," Jane acknowledged. "But I want to get this tied down without delay."

Mary Kate glanced over the seat at Stephanie and winked. That was the magic word. *Delay.*

"YOU SHOULD GIVE Joey a second chance." Valerie moved restlessly around Cole's kitchen, peeking under the lid of the meat container to sniff at the marinade, pressing a finger into a bread roll to test the freshness. "He's constantly dropping in for dinner because he can't afford to buy food. My grocery bill has tripled."

"Don't feed him," Cole said callously. "How else will he learn?"

"I have to feed him. He's my baby." Valerie dipped a pinkie into Cole's homemade salad dressing, tasted and frowned. "Garlic. Oh, Cole, you can't get close to people when you eat garlic. *Jane's* coming, remember."

"Sit down, Mum." Cole placed a glass of Pinot Grigio in her hand and shooed her into a chair. He didn't know what exasperated him more—his mother's attempts to interfere in his relationship with Jane, or with his carefully prepared barbecue. "Everything's under control."

"I could do more if only you'd let me." Valerie swiveled to watch him remove fresh salad greens from the fridge. She fidgeted with the charm on her wineglass.

"You made dessert, that's plenty," he said, deliberately ignoring her meaning. The fresh strawberry cheesecake taking up half the top shelf was indeed a major contribution.

"Are you really going to buy the farm?" Valerie asked.

"I'm trying to get the money together."

"Is Jane giving you a cheaper price? She ought to."

"I wouldn't expect that. She's helping me find a buyer for the Rasmussen estate. That's all the assistance I need from her."

"Deep down, Jane wants to be in Red Hill," Valerie insisted. "She just needs a reason to stay. You should try to talk her into it."

"She won't listen to me," Cole said over the sound of running water as he washed red and green lettuces. He shook them out and dumped them in a salad spinner. "Anyway, how can I get the farm if she stays in Red Hill?"

Valerie gave him a smile over her wineglass. "You two were sweet on each other once…"

Cole groaned. "Not you, too."

"Mary Kate's a lovely girl, isn't she?" Valerie said, wisely changing the subject. Picking up a knife, she started slicing radishes. "Stephanie hero-worships her. Such a pity she and Jane are moving."

"Melbourne is only an hour and a half away. The girls will still see each other."

Cole carefully took the knife from her. "Thanks, but I'm leaving the radishes whole."

"Whole? Are you sure?" Valerie's pursed lips showed him what she thought of that culinary gaffe. "It won't be the same as if they were living here and you know it."

He did. Instead of casually dropping in on his way past the farm to speak to Jane, he'd have to make an appointment. Instead of Mary Kate being able to come and go to and from his place at almost any time of the day, they'd have to plan the journey. Instead of having his family members around him, they'd be scattered.

The knife came down on the side of his thumb, drawing a thin line of red across the skin. He turned on the tap and stuck his finger beneath the stream of cold water. When had he started thinking of Jane and Mary Kate as family? Mary Kate, sure; she was his daughter. But Jane? Jane had let him know a long time ago that her independence was more important than family. "I'm applying for joint custody," Cole told his mother.

Valerie glanced up, eyebrows raised. "Oh, my. I thought you and Jane might agree to something less formal."

"I've tried." Cole turned off the water and wrapped a paper towel around his thumb. "She gets upset every time I raise the issue. I find it hard to keep my cool, as well. So I'm backing off. My lawyer is handling it."

"Dad!" Stephanie appeared in the doorway, holding his tux, still wrinkled from the last time he'd worn it—on his wedding day. "You need to get this cleaned for the premiere."

Cole frowned. "The what?"

"Stephanie, get your father a Band-Aid," Valerie said. "He's cut himself."

Stephanie nodded to her grandmother then turned back to Cole. "The *premiere*."

The doorbell rang.

"Put that back in my closet." Holding his injured hand in the air, Cole headed for the door.

"Pay attention, Dad," Stephanie said, running after him. "Jane wants you to go with her to the Australian premiere of *Swept Away*."

Cole stopped in the middle of the lounge room. He could see the silhouettes of Jane and Mary Kate behind the glass panel. "She hasn't said anything about it to me."

"She bought a fancy new dress. She wouldn't have done that unless she was going, would she?"

"Doesn't mean she's going with me."

Stephanie lifted her shoulders. "All I know is, five minutes after Mary Kate suggested she ask you, Jane decided to buy the dress."

The doorbell rang again.

"Put the tux away. And in the future, stay out of my closet." Cole waited until she'd moved off down the hall before opening the door. Was it true? Had Jane experienced a change of heart where he was concerned? Well, she would have to be the one to say something.

Jane, her blond hair hanging loosely around her shoulders, her slim figure shown to advantage in a knit wrap dress in cream with mocha piping, breezed in, carrying a plastic-covered platter. "I know you said not to bring anything but Mary

Kate begged me to make my Mexican layer dip."

Mary Kate greeted him with a sweet smile and handed him a bag of corn chips. "It's really good. She's a *fantastic* cook."

Jane squeezed her shoulder. "Thank you, sweetheart, but you don't have many other people to compare me to."

"Hello." Valerie entered the room, arms outstretched, her welcoming smile encompassing both Jane and Mary Kate. "It's lovely to see you both again."

"It's nice to see you." Jane hesitated, then leaned forward to kiss Valerie's cheek. "Mary Kate, do you remember Mrs. Roberts from the café?"

"Hi, Nanna." Mary Kate gave her grandmother a hug.

"My mother's been around quite a bit lately, seeing the girls," Cole explained when Jane looked surprised.

"We're old friends by now," Valerie said, smiling.

"We brought Mary Kate's baby photos to show you," Jane said to Valerie.

"Aw, Mom. She's not interested in a

bunch of old snapshots," Mary Kate complained. "I brought the computer disk with more recent pictures on it."

"Oh, my!" Valerie laughed. "These young people are so computer literate."

Jane shook her head. "Mary Kate is more savvy than I am. She even set up her own online bank account and a PayPal account. Using my credit card, of course."

"Let's look at the album first," Valerie suggested to Mary Kate. "We'll go through your life in chronological order." She moved over to the dark blue couch where Mary Kate joined her. Seeing Stephanie come into the room, she patted the cushion on her other side. "Give your father the Band-Aid and come and look at Mary Kate's photos with us."

"Come with me and we'll find a bowl for the chips," Cole said to Jane. "I have to finish the salad."

He led the way to the back to the kitchen and showed her the cupboard where the bowls were kept. Then, throwing the paper towel in the rubbish bin, he tried to pull at the tiny red string on the Band-Aid. It tore the wrong way and he swore under his breath. "Who do they think opens these things—pixies?" Laying it on the chopping board, he tried to whack the end off with his chef's knife.

"Let me." Using her nails, Jane tore the mangled Band-Aid wrapper off then removed the protective plastic on the sticky ends. She took his hand and started to apply the strip. That's where the operation stalled. The Band-Aid stuck to his thumb on one end but folded over on itself at the other end. Jane bent over his hand, her hair drifting across his skin, tickling like a silken feather. He felt her warm breath on his wrist and her cool fingers pressing into his flesh. Finally she peeled back the folded end and wound the strip around his thumb. "Whew! There you go."

"You forgot to kiss it better." At her startled expression, he winced. "Dumb thing to say."

With a faint smile, she held his gaze. Grasping his wrist, she raised it to her mouth and lightly touched her lips to his finger. "Anything else I can do for you?"

Adrenaline flooded his veins and for a moment he was speechless. Finally, he managed to say, "Give me a minute to catch my breath and I'll let you know." He poured her a glass of wine from the bottle in the cooler. "That's a switch from Miss Prickly Pear."

Her cheeks turned pink and she gave an embarrassed laugh. "I'm just in a good mood tonight. Feeling a bit reckless."

"What's brought that on?"

"I put in an offer on my apartment today." Jane peeled the plastic wrap off the dip platter. "Keep your fingers crossed for me that the vendor accepts it."

"They don't usually take the first offer," Cole said. "I hope you didn't give him your top bid."

"I didn't." She emptied the bag into a wooden bowl and put the bag in the bin. "I'm prepared to go higher, although it would be nice if I didn't have to."

"The first rule of real estate is, be prepared to walk away if the price is too high."

"I'll probably hear back over the

weekend," she said, climbing onto a bar stool. "Now that I've taken this step, I'll need a deposit check from you for the farm. It'll cover my deposit."

Cole felt a prickle of perspiration along his hairline. This whole deal was dicey until he tied down the Rasmussen estate. *If* he tied it down. "I've got a term deposit coming out next week. As soon as that money is in my account I'll give you a check."

"Fine. As you say, there'll be dickering back and forth on the apartment. We have a bit of time to play with. Oh, I finally got hold of Rafe. He's interested in talking to you about the property."

"Excellent." Cole held up his glass to toast. "To your apartment. And my vineyard."

Jane clinked glasses with him. Her skin up close was smooth and translucent, her blue eyes bright. It was hard sometimes to remember that he wasn't going to fall for her again.

The front door banged open and from the lounge room came the noise and commotion that attended only one person—his younger brother.

"Hey, Mama Bear, Little Bear dudes." Joey's booming voice was accompanied by a clinking of bottles and rustling of plastic bags. "Where's the man?"

CHAPTER NINE

COLE BRACED HIMSELF for the increase in decibel level as Joey entered the kitchen, closely followed by Crystal, Valerie and the girls. He hadn't seen Joey since he'd fired him, although he'd heard plenty from Valerie about what a hard time his brother was having.

"Hi, Crystal." He kissed his brother's girlfriend on the cheek. "I'm sorry about Joey losing his job."

Three years older than Joey, Crystal was the adult in their relationship. But they were both clearly smitten with each other. More than once Cole had envied what Joey and she had together.

"I don't blame *you*." Crystal ran a hand through her short brown curls. She winced as Joey haphazardly crashed his clinking plastic bag onto the counter. "He needed a jolt."

"Has it worked?"

"Not so far. But I'm on his case all the time." She reached into the pocket of her jeans. "I can pay you back some of the money—"

"No," Cole said, pushing her hand away. Crystal worked as a hairdresser and didn't have cash to spare. "He's got to learn to be responsible."

"Well, you're right." She glanced curiously at Jane and Mary Kate. "Is that your daughter and her mother?"

"Let me introduce you." Cole led her to where the others were grouped around the counter. "This is Crystal. Crystal, meet Jane, and my daughter, Mary Kate."

"Hey, dude, I hear congratulations are in order." Joey twisted off the wire cage covering the cork on a bottle of sparkling wine.

"What for?" Valerie asked, glancing hopefully from Cole to Jane.

"He's buying back Cockatoo Ridge."

At his brother's words, Cole felt a pang

of unease. Everyone was taking the deal for granted when he still didn't have the money. He'd always been cautious, never one to count his chickens. He'd hate if this blew up in his face.

"Will you plant a vineyard?" Jane asked.

"That's my plan, as soon as I can afford it," Cole admitted.

Twisting the cork out with a loud bang, Joey proceeded to fill any wineglass within reach.

Cole held his glass up to the bottle Joey was carelessly tilting. "Watch out. You're slopping that stuff all over."

Jane hastily downed the dregs of her Pinot Grigio before it got mixed with champagne. "Joey, I remember you as a pesky nine-year-old."

"Now I'm a pesky twenty-two-year-old." He spun without warning to tickle Stephanie in the ribs, sending her into paroxysms of giggles. To Mary Kate, he said, "You must be my new niece."

"And you're my wicked uncle Joey!" Mary Kate said, clearly thrilled.

"I *am* rather depraved," Joey admitted

modestly. "But only on weekends and public holidays."

"Don't tease, she'll take you seriously." Cole rescued the bottle and poured a glass for Valerie and Crystal.

"Now that you're going to start your own vineyard," Joey said, "when do I take over the real estate office?"

"In your dreams, mate." *He* was dreaming if he'd thought his brother would act abashed. But what the hell, Cole was glad they had the sort of relationship where they could say anything to each other. "Where's that money you owe me?"

"Now, Cole." Valerie's glance flitted uneasily between her sons. "I'm sure Joey will pay you back when he can."

"Too right, dude." Grinning, Joey pulled a bundle of notes from his pants pocket with a flourish. "Ta da!" He threw a sheepish glance at Crystal, who looked surprised.

"Thanks. I think," Cole said, "this can only be winnings at the slots." Faking a jab to Joey's ribs, Cole got him in a headlock, only partly joking around. "No more gambling. You promised."

"And you believed me!" Joey scuffled, feinted and wriggled out, his dark hair sticking up and his shirt twisted.

"Joey, Joey!" Stephanie got hold of his arm and bounced up and down. "Come outside and see what Mary Kate and I have been practicing with the horses. We're doing barrel racing."

"Go ahead," Cole said. "You've got time before I start the barbecue."

"Will you come and watch, too, Nanna?" Mary Kate asked.

"I'd love to." Valerie put an arm around Mary Kate's shoulders and followed Stephanie and Joey. "Coming, Crystal?"

The girls ran out the door. Joey teased his nieces volubly all the way across the yard to the stable. Crystal and Valerie followed more sedately, talking quietly.

"Whew," Jane said. "Talk about a whirlwind."

"Never a dull moment when Joey's around." Cole sprinkled the radishes around the edges of the salad. He put the platter on the table and set a jar of dressing next to it. "Stephanie was over the moon after her shopping trip with you yesterday."

"She picked up some great bargains."

"According to her logic she saved me a heap of money," he said dryly. "I understand *you* got a new dress."

Jane's eyes lit. "It's utterly self-indulgent but absolutely divine. To justify the expense I've been telling myself it's not every day I go to a red-carpet event."

"It's special, all right." He waited but she said nothing more about inviting him to the premiere. Had Stephanie got it wrong? Then shrugging it off, he said, "The food's ready. I'll give them a few minutes before I turn on the barbecue."

Jane moved to the window where she could see the paddock. "Do you want to go watch?"

Cole looked over Jane's shoulder. Joey, Crystal and Valerie were leaning against the fence while Mary Kate and Stephanie saddled the horses. He would enjoy being with them all.

But Jane's hair smelled of orchards, and the nape of her neck was visible where she'd pushed her hair to one side. "Why don't we go into the other room and you can show me photos of Mary Kate as a baby."

JANE FELT the cushion sink under Cole's weight as he sat down, so close his thigh rested against hers. He stretched one arm along the couch back behind her and leaned in to look at the album between them. She identified the photos automatically, too aware of his solid warmth next to her to be able to think straight.

"You didn't see any of these when I came back for a visit when Mary Kate was five?" she asked.

"One or two. Not a whole album full." He glanced down at her. "As I recall, you spent most of your time with your aunt."

"I let you see Mary Kate as often as you were able to," Jane rejoined. "That's all you wanted."

Ignoring that, Cole flipped slowly through the photos. "She was a cute kid."

"She was extremely precocious. But then, she still is." Jane turned to a photo taken when Mary Kate was about four. "Valerie told me you had asthma as a child."

"Yes. I outgrew it." Cole started to turn the page then stopped. "Did Mary Kate have asthma?"

Jane nodded, shivering. "It was pretty scary. The first time she had an attack I was at the film studio. The babysitter called the ambulance and they took her to the hospital. I died a thousand deaths getting there."

"Does she still have a problem?" Cole asked, frowning. "You should have told me, in case something happened."

"She's grown out of it, too. She doesn't even use an inhaler anymore."

"That's a relief." Cole turned another page of the album. Mary Kate, age about six, was holding a Maltese puppy close to her chest and beaming out at the camera. "She looks pretty pleased with herself."

"Too smart for her own good," Jane said, chuckling. "Before we got this dog she spent half a day arguing that a child whose mother worked needed a pet. I agreed in principle and straightaway she went next door and came home with Moppet. Free to a good home."

Cole laughed. "Did you let her keep him?"

"Yes. And to her credit she looked after the dog herself. Unfortunately we had to leave Moppet in L.A. because of the strict quarantine laws here." Jane looked back to the photo and shook her head. "I was upset because she'd gone next door without my knowing about it."

"Stephanie used to play all up and down the street," Cole said. "Now she roams for miles on her horse. Different environment, I suppose. I know everyone around here. It's too bad—"

"Too bad I didn't raise Mary Kate in Red Hill?" Jane threw him a glance, her mouth twisted. She turned a page and a loose photo fell out. It was of herself at age eight standing between her father and mother.

"Are those your parents?" Cole asked.

She nodded, swallowing hard, and tucked the photo deep in the back of the album.

"You have never told me what happened to them."

She didn't really want to tell him now, but somehow she found herself doing so. It had been so long since she'd spoken of them. Only Esther and Mary Kate knew the full story.

"Two weeks after that photo was taken they went on a trip to Queensland." Jane blinked back the tears that threatened to spill and took a deep breath. "It was their first holiday alone since I was born. While they were there they went scuba diving on the Great Barrier Reef. They went out but for some reason, the boat didn't pick them up. Forgot them, I guess, in the crowd of tourists. The tour guide motored in to the shore without them. It was miles out, too far for them to swim back."

"What, your parents were just left out there on the reef?" Cole said, appalled. "Wasn't there a search?"

Jane nodded, biting her lip to control the tremble. "Eventually, when their absence was discovered. Their bodies were never found. No one knows what happened to them. The tour operator was found to be negligent, but that couldn't bring them back."

"Oh, Jane." He pulled her into his embrace.

Jane sank against his chest, aware of his warmth and strength. As her tears seeped into his shirt, she felt her pent-up grief release. She raised her face, meaning to thank him, but her words flew out of her mind. His eyes held compassion and something darker, something so strong it took away her breath. Suddenly Jane longed, not for the teenage boy who'd betrayed her, but for the man Cole had become. And in the same flash of insight she knew he was attracted, too—and fighting it just as hard as she was.

He leaned closer. She should pull away but somehow she couldn't. Then he kissed her. And her willpower crumbled. She pulled him closer again, craving the comfort of his chest, the strength of his arms around her. He deepened the kiss, angling his mouth, and she recognized his taste, his texture.

A noise from the kitchen brought self-preservation flooding back. She drew away, suddenly aware of what she'd done. Letting down her guard like that. Kissing him. She was fooling herself. Cole was the same man he'd always been.

Pressing her hand against his chest, she savored the beat of his heart one last second before she pushed him away. "Wow," she said. "That wine really hit me hard."

The light in Cole's eyes clouded. His voice hardened. "It can have that effect." He listened a moment to the hubbub in the kitchen. "The hordes have returned."

"SO I SAID TO Mrs. Terpstra, if you come down a couple of thousand dollars, you can move into the retirement village next month." Joey waved his wineglass so that the red sloshed up the curved sides. "And I told the buyer, if you go up a couple of thousand, the house is yours." He sat back and glanced around the table. "Everybody was happy. I love that."

"Welcome to Real Estate 101," Cole

murmured humorously. Joey was young enough and new enough at realty to think he'd invented the art of negotiation, but Cole had to admit his brother did have a knack for bringing people to the table. "If you were as enthusiastic about showing up on time and doing the paperwork as you are about talking to people, you'd make a really good agent."

Joey pushed aside his empty plate and leaned over the table and the platter containing scraps of barbecued lamb. "Give me another chance. I'll toe the line and do all the boring stuff. Promise."

"Please, Daddy," Stephanie begged. "Give Uncle Joey his job back."

"Yes, please do," Mary Kate joined in the appeal.

Cole eyed the pair askance. "Did Joey put you two up to this?"

"No," they both said at once.

Cole glanced at Joey. He was grinning and showing off, enjoying his cheering squad's efforts. But when he looked at Cole there was a vulnerable plea in his eyes that showed Cole he was anything but confident. Their father had asked Cole on his deathbed to look out for Joey. He'd done his best, but sometimes it wasn't clear what the right course of action was. "Give me one good reason why I should rehire him?"

Stephanie looked first at Mary Kate, who nodded, then at Joey. "Because he said that next time he was flush he'd take me and Mary Kate to Luna Park."

Cole snorted. "He's been promising you Luna Park since you were five years old. By the time he gets around to it, you'll be too old for roller coasters and Ferris wheels. What makes you think he would follow through this time?"

"My word is my bond," Joey proclaimed.

"Maybe, but *I'm* going to get it in writing." Mary Kate produced a piece of loose-leaf paper with a few lines of hand-written text on it and passed it down the table. "This is a contract. Both of you have to sign."

Jane picked it up and read, "'I, Joey Roberts, promise to take my nieces to Luna Park at any convenient date in the next two months if Cole Roberts gives me my job back. I, Cole Roberts, promise to rehire Joey if he stops gambling.' There are places for two signatures." Laughing, Jane handed the document across to Cole. "I'm afraid this looks legally binding."

Cole scanned the contract. Joey could be aggravating, but he'd missed having him around the office. Surely looking out for him meant giving him another chance when he screwed up.

"What do you say, dude?" Joey stopped clowning around and his expression was dead serious. "Give me another go?"

"Do it, Cole," Valerie urged. "He's your brother."

"Oh, all right." Cole took the pen Mary Kate held out and wrote his signature in neat flowing script on the paper. He passed the paper to Joey. "This is your last chance. Make sure you behave."

Joey grabbed the pen and scrawled his name below Cole's. "You won't regret this."

COLE WAITED all evening for Jane to bring up the movie premiere. Valerie left and then Joey and Crystal. The girls had gone to Stephanie's room, from which muffled laughter erupted now and then. Jane was murmuring how she'd better be going, so he made her a last cup of coffee. Maybe she'd forgotten. Maybe he'd scared her off with that kiss. God, what had he been thinking? Well, that's just it. He hadn't thought, he'd acted on impulse, one that had been building since the day she'd waltzed into his office and asked him to sell Cockatoo Ridge.

"I got my tux out to be cleaned," Cole said, passing her the cream. "Or I should say, Stephanie did. She can stay at her mother's the night of the premiere. If you don't have other arrangements for Mary Kate, Leslie probably wouldn't mind taking her, as well."

"I beg your pardon?" Jane frowned over the top of her cup. "What are you talking about?"

"The premiere," he said patiently. "The gala event you bought a new dress for. You wanted me to escort you."

Jane's eyebrows rose. "Since when?"

The penny dropped. Cole set his cup down so hard the hot liquid slopped over and burned his hand. "Those girls have done it again. Stephanie said you were going to ask me to the premiere."

"I don't know where they got that idea." Jane put aside her coffee, too. "I distinctly told Mary Kate that I *wasn't* going to ask you."

"I clean up as well as the next guy, you know," Cole said. "We're not hicks down here in Red Hill."

"Oh, for goodness' sake, it's not that. We agreed we weren't going to get railroaded into going out together."

"Glitzy events and crowds of strangers aren't my thing, anyway," Cole said. "I only brought up the subject because Stephanie seemed to think it would be a good idea. But if you don't need me—"

"I don't need any favors." She put her cup down and reached behind a chair for her purse. "I really have to go. Thank you for dinner. I had a great time."

"I'll call the girls." Cole went down the hall to Stephanie's bedroom, knocked and opened the door. Mary Kate slammed the phone down, her expression frozen. She turned to Stephanie and they both burst into laughter.

"What are you two up to?" he asked, suspicious.

"Nothing," they said simultaneously and burst into giggles all over again.

"The phone is not a toy." They were probably calling boys and hanging up. He'd have to speak to Stephanie about that later.

Jane appeared at his side. "Mary Kate, we're going."

Amid the predictable moans and groans, Cole walked Jane out to the front steps. The girls ran past them to the car.

"I appreciate your being willing to go with me," Jane told him. "But you can see how impossible it is."

"Not a problem." He brushed aside the unexpected twinge of disappointment, reminding himself it wasn't his sort of thing anyway.

She was halfway down the walk when she stopped and retraced her steps. "I've changed my mind. I want you to come to the premiere. In fact, you'd be perfect."

"In what way?" he asked, wary at her abrupt change of heart.

"As Mia's date."

"Mia MacDonald? Is that the actress in the movie you're promoting?" Cole brushed a hand through his hair then immediately smoothed it down again. "I don't think I've ever seen her in anything. Why are you setting me up with her? Is she too unattractive to get her own date?"

Jane hooted with laughter. "What planet have you been hiding on? Mia is the next Catherine Zeta-Jones. Ask Stephanie if you don't believe me."

"Then why me?"

"She doesn't like walking the red carpet alone and asked me to find her an escort. Someone handsome and tall, strong and kind—"

"You're sucking up." He crossed his arms over his chest.

"Okay," Jane conceded. "She wants someone who won't attract more attention than her but who's hot enough to make her look good."

"In other words, a handbag," Cole said flatly.

"A *gorgeous* handbag."

"You're setting me up with an overrated starlet. I may not be familiar with Mia but I know her type from the movie magazines in my doctor's waiting room. Who are *you* going with?"

"Rafe. He declined to go with Mia."

"I'm betting he has a good reason."

"What's wrong with you?" Jane demanded. "Mia was voted the fifth sexiest woman alive by *People* magazine. Any red-blooded male would jump at a chance to escort her to a dog show, much less a film premiere."

What *was* wrong with him? Maybe what he chafed at was the idea of Jane going with Rafe. "A celebrity is hardly the kind of father figure you want for Mary Kate."

Jane threw up her hands. "Rafe is just an old friend. There's no question of him becoming a surrogate father to Mary

Kate." She came closer and tucked a finger inside his shirt. "This will be your chance to talk to him about the Rasmussen estate."

"There is that." Cole reconsidered. "Okay, when is it?"

"Next Saturday." Jane was all business now, jotting down notes to herself on a pad she'd pulled out of her purse as she outlined the logistics of the "date." "We can drive together to the hotel I've booked as a base for the night. We'll pick Rafe and Mia up at their hotels in a limo and ride together to the theater. After the premiere there's a private party at a restaurant in the city. You'll attend that with Mia, as I will with Rafe."

Cole shook his head, dazed at the speed with which she'd organized events. Then he glanced at the car. Stephanie and Mary Kate were both inside with the door open and the light on, heads bent together. "What are they up to now?"

"Not more matchmaking, I hope." Jane put her notebook away. "About that kiss earlier."

"What about it?"

"The predominant emotion was grief on my part," she explained. "We'd been looking at the album and I was feeling sad about my parents and you were consoling me. I kissed you back even though I knew I shouldn't because—"

"Whoa, whoa, whoa," Cole said, holding up his hands. "Let's *not* dissect that kiss, shall we? We don't have to verbalize *everything*."

Jane pushed his hand away. "How else will you know what I'm thinking? Or understand me? And vice versa."

"I'm quite content for you to view me as a man of mystery," he said, peeved and amused at the same time. "I really didn't need to know that you only kissed me because you felt sad."

"Well, that might not be the *only* reason…"

"Ah…"

"I was curious whether you still kissed the same."

That sounded promising. "Do I?"

Now her mouth curled up and her eyes danced. "No."

"So what's different?" He took a step closer.

"As you said, why dissect the kiss? We're not going to repeat it, so there's no point." She backed down the step, waggling her fingers in farewell. "I'll call you."

"Sure," Cole replied dryly. "We'll do lunch."

CHAPTER TEN

CHLORINE FUMES hit Jane's nostrils as she entered the swimming-pool complex, triggering humiliating memories of high school swim meets where she'd come last in every event.

"Are you sure you want your bronze medallion?" she asked, trailing after Mary Kate. "You don't have to do everything Stephanie does if you're not interested."

"It's not me who doesn't like sports, Mom. It's you." Mary Kate, clutching her towel, spotted Stephanie with her mother on the bleachers beside the pool, and waved. "There they are."

Leslie wore the glow of perfection Jane remembered so well. Her blond pageboy gleamed and a light cardigan was casually draped over her cornflower-blue sundress.

She was pretty, pleasant and popular, a genuinely nice person. Everyone liked Leslie.

Mary Kate ran ahead. Jane followed slowly. A small knot of youngsters in bathing suits had gathered at the far end, their chatter echoing beneath the high ceiling. Mary Kate had her bathing suit on under her clothes. She stripped off her shorts and T-shirt, tossed them onto the bench, then she and Stephanie hurried over to join the other swimmers.

"Hi, Leslie!" Jane heard her own voice, high-pitched and overly bright. Just like that, she was thirteen again, the new girl in town, the *weird* one who didn't play sports and would rather watch movies than hang out at the footy grounds. If she'd stayed in Red Hill, if Cole hadn't gone back to Leslie, things might have been different. But she hadn't, he had, and nothing had changed. Odd how years could pass and she was perfectly content with who she was, yet she still felt the odd one out.

"Hello, Jane." In contrast, Leslie's voice was quiet and well modulated. Her smile was calm and confident, not brazen and challenging. She was, if anything, more attractive than she'd been in high school. "It's good to see you again."

Leslie seemed to have gotten over any ill feeling she might have had that Cole had so quickly found solace in Jane's arms after their high school breakup. Then again, why should she harbor a grudge? She'd gotten him back when she needed him. Jane checked her mean thoughts. The galling truth was, Leslie must be rather special if Cole had loved her.

Jane sank onto the bench a couple of feet away, her legs angled awkwardly by the narrow space. She checked her mobile to make sure it was on. Jason could call any time about the apartment. Then she tucked it away in her purse. "How've you been? What have you been doing this past decade?"

"Raising kids mostly," Leslie told her with a self-deprecating smile. "Once Stephanie started school I got my teaching degree. Now that Fergus's boys are in kindergarten I'm working part-time at the primary school. What about you? I hear you're a movie publicist."

"That's right," Jane said. "I transferred from L.A. to the Melbourne office of Moonray Productions."

"It must be so exciting to work with celebrities." Leslie shivered with delight. "What are they really like?"

"They're the same as anybody else," Jane said. "Except that they get whatever they want, whenever they want."

Leslie laughed. "You were always so funny."

"You think so?" Jane fingered her amber beads, surprised Leslie had even known she existed except as the girl who'd briefly distracted Cole.

"I'm really sorry about your aunt." Leslie leaned over, touching Jane's arm. Her voice was soft, her hazel eyes warm with concern. "I know how much she missed you."

"How would you know that?" Jane blurted.

"I used to visit her."

Jane blinked. "You did?"

"I loved her pottery," Leslie said. "I bought some of her smaller pieces as gifts for people. I wish I'd gotten something for myself before it was too late."

Jane recalled seeing her at Esther's funeral and wondering what she'd been doing there. Maybe it was the words *too late* or that Leslie had known her aunt. Suddenly Jane opened up. "I miss Aunt Esther. We saw each other almost every year when she flew to L.A., but it was never enough. It always seemed so rushed."

"I used to go up to the farm and watch her work when Stephanie was little," Leslie told her. "I think she enjoyed talking to me because I was your age and Stephanie was Mary Kate's age."

"You always think there's plenty of time," Jane went on almost as if Leslie wasn't there. "Then somehow the years slip away. The last time I saw her, I said, 'We'll be over next Christmas.' But Mary Kate got chicken pox and we didn't come. Then another year passed and another."

"Esther was such an interesting woman," Leslie mused. "She was passionate about her work but she knew how to enjoy the simple things in life." Leslie patted Jane's knee. "Independent, like you."

"I never expected her to…die so soon." Jane's voice trembled. She'd been so caught up in the move back home, dealing with her aunt's effects and coming to grips with Cole's claim on Mary Kate that she hadn't had time to grieve for Esther.

Leslie moved along the bench and put an arm around Jane. "It was the same with my grandmother who lived with us. She taught me to crochet and bake. She convinced my mum to let me get my ears pierced when I was only ten. She was always there when I came home from school. Nanna died when I was fifteen but I still cry when I think of her. I know how terrible it feels to lose someone you love."

Jane felt like a hypocrite because the comfort was so welcome. She fumbled in her purse for something to dry her eyes. "I'm sorry. I can't believe I'm blubbering away in a swimming-pool complex and telling *you* my woes. Damn it, where are those tissues?"

Leslie handed her some from her own purse. "Why shouldn't you tell me? We've known each other for years, maybe not as well as we could have. But we have someone we love in common."

Jane snapped back to reality with a short humorless laugh. "You mean Cole?"

"Actually, I meant Esther."

"Oh." Jane buried her face in the tissues. "I'm glad she had your company. She didn't seek out people as a rule. I just wonder why she never told me about you."

"Maybe because she thought you'd be upset because of Cole."

"I don't know why," Jane blustered. "Cole wasn't anything to me, not really."

"You just told me you loved him," Leslie said gently.

Jane froze, unable to think of what to say. Then splashing in the pool caught their attention and she didn't have to answer. The water churned with children swimming freestyle toward the far end. Stephanie was in second place, Mary Kate second last. Jane leaned forward, her hands curled around the edge of the bench.

"Come on, sweetheart," she urged. "You can do it!"

"You do know it's not a race, don't you?" Leslie said, amused. "They're doing warm-up laps."

"Really? Oh." Jane sat back, tucking her hair behind her ear. "Warm-up laps. Right." She was such an idiot.

"I loved him, too, back then," Leslie said, sighing. "At least I thought I did."

"And Cole loved you," Jane said flatly.

Leslie glanced sideways at her. "He carried the responsibilities of a man on his shoulders, even though he was only eighteen. We did what our families expected of us."

Jane's silence lasted several painful beats of her heart. Was her archrival telling her the man they'd both loved had only married her out of duty? But Leslie didn't know what Jane knew. "There was more to his decision than that."

Leslie shrugged and her cardigan slipped. Pulling it up, she added, "That's all I know. And I lived with him for years."

Jane glanced back to the pool. The kids

had turned around and were halfway to the other end. Mary Kate was in second place. It might not be a race but Mary Kate was doing okay.

"By the way," Leslie said, "a group of us are trying to revive the Red Hill Little Theater. We would love to have someone with your acting experience to play the female lead. Would you be interested?"

It had been years since she'd done any acting, but just the suggestion brought a surge of excitement. With regret Jane quashed it. "I'm sorry, I couldn't. I'm moving to the city soon."

"So you *are* going. That's too bad. Stephanie was really hoping Mary Kate would start high school with her."

"They'll see each other on weekends. I promised Mary Kate I'd bring her out every Saturday until she finishes her bronze medallion."

"I'm sorry, too," Leslie said. "That we won't get to know each other better. In high school we were so trapped in our cliques."

Jane watched the kids swimming for a few minutes in silence. "I get movie passes," she said at last and glanced at Leslie. "We could go together, if you like."

"I'd love that." Leslie's eyes shone. "It would be wonderful to talk about a movie with someone who's close to the business." A whistle blew and she looked across to the pool. "They're finished for today. If you'll excuse me, I need to talk to the coach. But I'll see you next time."

"I look forward to it," Jane said and realized she really would. She rose and gathered up Mary Kate's things. Leslie started down the rows of seats. Jane caught up and tentatively put a hand on her shoulder. "Thanks for being so nice to my aunt."

Leslie pulled her into a hug. "Go easy on yourself. You need time to grieve."

"I will," Jane said, hugging her back. "I'm sorry about your grandmother."

Mary Kate came running over, arms tight to her sides, grinning madly. "Mom, did you see me?"

"You were great." Jane handed her a towel and waved goodbye to Leslie. "Do you want to get changed here?"

"Okay." She gathered up her clothes and headed for the change rooms. "Can Stephanie come back with us? Her mom has to go shopping."

"Yes." Jane sat down again to wait and to think. Leslie had been as much a victim of circumstance as she had been. And Cole. But Cole had said what he'd said knowing Jane would be devastated. There was no way he could have loved her.

The scary thing was, she was starting to fall for him again. No matter what malarkey she'd told him about that kiss, her response had arisen from sheer longing for him. She couldn't let that happen again. She had to keep her emotions under control, not let him see how she felt, no matter how difficult it was. If she failed, she could get hurt again. If he hadn't loved her then, why would he love her now? Mary Kate was who he really wanted.

She was so lost in thought she didn't hear her phone until it rang six times. Scrambling in her purse, she clicked it on. "Hello? Jason. Any news?"

"I'm sorry, but late last night I received

a phone call from someone wanting to make an offer on the apartment," he said. "For the full price of seven-fifty."

"Oh, no!" Jane clapped a hand to her forehead. "Now what?"

"The other buyer has to sign a contract note and put down a small deposit to secure the deal," Jason said. "You have twenty-four hours to beat their offer."

"And then?"

"The vendor will accept the highest bid."

"IS IT POSSIBLE the agent is simply putting a hard sell on me?" Jane asked Cole. She'd gone straight from the swimming pool to his office to talk over the problem. She respected Cole's experience and good judgment. But more than that, she wanted him on her side as a trusted friend. Pacing in front of his desk, she demanded, "Who offers the asking price?"

"Those for whom money is no object," Cole replied. "*If* the agent is trying to force you up, it's highly unethical, although strictly speaking, not illegal."

Jane glanced out the glass wall to the

lobby. The girls' wet heads were bent together over a magazine. "To get the apartment, I have to stump up another seventy-five thousand, minimum." Pausing, she asked, "Is there any way to check if the other offer was real?"

Cole leaned back in his chair. "Walk away. If Jason doesn't have another legitimate offer, he'll soon be calling you back. If, on the other hand, he does…"

"I lose out," Jane said flatly. "And it's too late."

"I could call him and see what I can find out."

"Would you?" Jane dropped into a chair. "He might say things to another agent he wouldn't say to a buyer."

Cole reached for the phone. "Do you have the number?"

Jane handed him the card with Jason's mobile number. After a few minutes of agent-to-agent chitchat, Cole asked how strong interest was in the apartment. "Oh, really. I see." To Jane, he nodded. *Someone really made an offer.*

Jane tapped the arm of her chair, wondering where she was going to get another seventy-five thousand dollars.

Suddenly Cole jerked upright. "No!"

Jane stopped tapping.

He dragged a hand over his face. "*Cherry Magoo?* You've got to be kidding."

"What!" Jane shrieked. This was not happening.

"Look, mate, I happen to know that person," Cole said into the phone, waving a hand to shush Jane. "She's not a genuine buyer. Trust me on this. Didn't she sound rather young? Elderly, really? If you have any other offers on the table, I would go with them. Okay, you'll find out when she doesn't show up with the dough."

He hung up, shaking his head.

"My own daughter," Jane exclaimed. "She's deliberately trying to sabotage me."

Cole went to the door. "Stephanie! Mary Kate! Get in here. Now!"

Stephanie paled and hung back. Mary Kate marched in with her chin up, standing slightly in front of Stephanie as if to protect her sister.

"I've just been talking to the agent

who's handling the Docklands apartment sale. Cherry Magoo. What kind of a prank did you two think you were playing?" Cole demanded.

Stephanie mumbled something unintelligible. Mary Kate maintained a determined silence.

"You've created a serious problem for Jane," Cole went on. "Potentially costing her tens of thousands of dollars and possibly losing the apartment she wants so badly. On top of that you lied to a complete stranger and pretended to be someone you aren't. That's called fraud."

"Mary Kate, what were you thinking?" Jane broke in. "You *know* how important that apartment is to me."

"I don't want to live there," Mary Kate said, unrepentant.

Cole turned to Stephanie. "What do *you* have to say for yourself?"

She shrugged miserably, casting a flickering sideways glance at Mary Kate, confirming Jane's suspicion that her daughter had been the instigator. "We had a good reason?"

"What reason could be good enough to lie?" Jane asked.

Stephanie started to speak, but Mary Kate elbowed her into silence.

"What made you think you could get away with such a ridiculous scheme?" Cole demanded, looking from Mary Kate to Stephanie. "You must know you'd never be able to pull it off, that you'd have to show up in person to sign a contract note and hand over money."

"We only wanted to delay the sale," Stephanie said.

Again, Mary Kate nudged her to keep quiet.

"I don't understand how Jason could have been fooled into thinking a young girl was an adult," Jane said.

"Mary Kate can do impersonations," Stephanie explained, full of admiration. "She pretended to be a rich widow from Florida."

"*Stephanie,*" Mary Kate groaned in exasperation. "Be quiet."

Cole turned to Jane. "We'll have to punish them."

"I agree," Jane said. "No horseback riding for a week."

"What!" Mary Kate and Stephanie cried in unison. "We're sorry."

"Too little," Jane said, arms crossed.

"Too late," Cole added. "You girls will work either here in the office, or at the farm. You'll be under close watch, unable to get into trouble."

"You can start tomorrow, cleaning out the barn where Aunt Esther kept her pottery materials," Jane added.

Mary Kate groaned loudly, her shoulders slumping. "There are huge chunks of clay in there. They're really heavy."

"Good," Jane said, unmoved. "You'll build muscles for the future when you're doing hard time."

MARY KATE HEAVED the last bag of unused clay off the shelving in the barn and dropped it in the wheelbarrow to be trundled off to the garage and deposited among the ever-growing collection of items to be disposed of.

"Let's take a break." Mary Kate sat

cross-legged on an ancient bale of hay. Dust motes climbed the beam of sunlight that filtered through the door.

The pottery wheel was too heavy for them to move and the kiln would have to be dismantled by grown-ups. There were tools and glazes and shards of fired and unfired pottery left to gather up. Mary Kate turned over a sky-blue vase she'd found at the back of a shelf. Scarcely big enough to hold a single flower, it was the prettiest thing she'd ever seen. And she meant to keep it.

"Did you ever meet your mum's aunt?" Stephanie asked, swiveling the backless seat attached to the pottery wheel.

"Lots of times," Mary Kate replied. "She was neat. She told me to call her Esther and talked to me as if I was a grown-up."

Stephanie picked at the dried clay on the frame of the wheel. "My mum often brought me with her when she came to visit. Esther would always give me a lump of clay to work with. She showed me how to make a pinch pot and other stuff."

"She told my mom one time she would

raise me," Mary Kate said. "So Mom could have her dream of being an actress."

"We would have been friends a long time ago."

"Yeah, but then I wouldn't have had Mom." Mary Kate cradled the vase in her hands and paced across the dusty floor. "Life is so *random*."

"I know." Stephanie slowly set the wheel spinning with her feet. "Things aren't turning out the way we hoped with Dad and Jane. Putting a phony bid on the apartment was a bad idea. It didn't slow things down for long and we got into trouble."

"We had to do something." Mary Kate kicked at a broken piece of unfired pottery. "We have to do *more*. Everything's happening too quickly. They haven't had time to fall in love again."

"There's still the premiere," Stephanie said, chewing on the end of her ponytail. "Too bad they're both going with other people."

"Mom and Rafe are just friends," Mary Kate said dismissively. "Mia's hot but I've noticed Mom grinds her teeth every time she calls. I think she must be a pain in the butt. Mom and Cole *might* turn to each other for consolation during the night. But we can't bank on it. We need a plan B."

"Once your mum hands over the deposit and signs a contract note, it's pretty much a done deal," Stephanie said. "Unless there are liens on the property or the financing falls through."

"How do you know all this?" Mary Kate asked.

"Dad's a real estate agent. He and Uncle Joey talk about this crap all the time."

"So how do we stop the deal from happening?"

"Well," Stephanie said, "Dad's giving her a check as a deposit on the farm. She's going to use that money to pay *her* deposit on the apartment. I heard him telling Nanna about it."

"So all we have to do is stop his money from getting to Mom," Mary Kate said thoughtfully. "With no deposit for her apartment, the deal will fall through. She'll be stuck with the farm. I'll get my horse and we'll go shopping every second weekend."

"But how are you to stop her from getting Dad's money?" Stephanie asked.

Mary Kate scuffed her sneakered toe on the dusty floor, thinking hard. Then she glanced up with a big smile. "Wicked Uncle Joey."

Stephanie stopped kicking the wheel. Her feet, resting on top, acted as brakes with a scraping noise. "Joey won't help us. He's in enough trouble already."

"Exactly," Mary Kate said. "But he won't even know he's helping us."

"What are you talking about?"

"I don't know," Mary Kate admitted. "But something will come to me. It always does."

CHAPTER ELEVEN

COLE ADJUSTED his black tie in the bedroom mirror and combed his hair neatly to one side. Red-carpet galas weren't his usual Saturday-night entertainment, but he'd show Jane he was no hick.

Squinting at his teeth, he tried on a star-dazzling smile. Or so he hoped. "Cole Roberts, good evening." Nope, too formal. "Hi, I'm Cole." Too boyish. He lowered his voice to strong and sexy. "I'm Cole. How are *you* tonight?"

A slow hand clap from the doorway brought heat rushing to Cole's cheeks. He spun around.

Elegant and amused, Jane stood in the doorway wearing a shimmering evening gown that took his breath away. Her hair glittered, her skin glistened, and as she walked toward him, he was enveloped in a delicate scent that was both sweet and sensual.

"You can't go like that," she said, eyeing him with critical detachment.

"What's wrong?" He turned back to the mirror. "I thought I scrubbed up pretty good."

"Your tux fits as if it was custom-made, you're handsome enough to turn a starlet's head, but—"

"It's the growth, isn't it?" he said, rubbing the stubble he'd been cultivating for a couple of days. "Stephanie and Mary Kate insisted, Joey agreed and stupidly I listened. Do I have time to shave?"

"The beard is sexy. If you like that sort of thing," she quickly amended. She turned him around by the shoulders to study him at closer range, tapping a polished fingernail against luscious berry-red lips. He was focusing on those lips, feeling their magnetism, when she murmured, "That's it," and reached up to tousle his hair.

"Hey!" he cried, ducking. Too late. Her fingers had tousled his neatly combed hair into a rumpled, spiky look. He was reaching for his comb, when he stopped. Okay, not bad. Less professional but more youthful. There was something intimate about her helping him get ready. He met her gaze in the mirror.

Heat flashed in her eyes, so briefly he thought he'd imagined it. Then she glanced away with a careless murmur. "You'll do."

He reminded himself this wasn't a date but a business opportunity. He was going for the sole purpose of selling property to Rafe.

The sound of whispering made him glance across the room. Stephanie and Mary Kate were crowding the doorway.

"Smile!" Stephanie said, holding up a camera. She clicked and captured him and Jane in profile. "You two look awesome together."

"Turn around so we can get a photo face-on," Mary Kate instructed. "Closer. Put your arms around each other's waists."

"Humor them," Cole murmured, sliding his arm around Jane. "We'll get this over with faster than if we argue."

She edged over, holding herself stiffly as

if she couldn't bear to get close to him. Cole put on a smile for the camera and settled his hand on the curve of her hip. It felt too damn good there, sparking memories he'd do better to forget and recent fantasies he had no business indulging in. "Hurry up, Stephanie."

Twenty shots or so later, he declared, "Enough! You'd think we were a couple of teenagers going to their first deb ball."

Stephanie and Mary Kate giggled and melted away like a pair of conjoined twins, squabbling good-naturedly as they reviewed the shots they'd just taken.

Once the girls had left, the sudden silence became awkward. Cole held out an arm to Jane and tried on his killer smile. "Shall we go?"

"Save it for Mia." Jane sailed out ahead of him.

But as he helped her tuck her skirt into the passenger seat of his car, his hand brushed her bare shoulder. She started, her eyes flying to his, lips parted. Then she turned away. His heart humming, Cole carefully closed the door.

JANE SIPPED her champagne and silently fumed. They were at the exclusive restaurant Moonray Productions had booked for the premiere after party. Mia was draped all over Cole on the far side of the dining table, and he wasn't doing a thing to undrape her. Jane appreciated his helping her out, but he didn't have to enjoy it so much. Mia was fawning over Cole as if *he* were the celebrity and she an adoring fan.

Rafe tilted the bottle of Bollinger to refill Jane's flute. "So this is the bloke who knocked you up with Mary Kate. Would you like me to get my stuntman to beat him up for you?"

"It's a little late for that." Jane sipped her wine then scrunched her nose as the bubbles tickled. "Thanks anyway."

"You still have a thing for him." Rafe tsked, shaking his craggy, handsome face. "You should never have given him to Mia."

"You're not allowed to smoke in here," she complained, stubbing out his butt in the saucer he'd commandeered for an ashtray. "I don't have a thing for Cole. And he's only on loan to Mia."

Rafe pulled a fresh cigarette from the pack. "That's not what Mia thinks."

It had started hours ago, outside the hotel where they'd picked up Mia. Leaving Rafe and Cole in the limo, Jane had gone up to get the actress. She was still in her dressing gown, leisurely applying her makeup. Once she'd grilled Jane about Cole and found out she was being escorted by a real estate agent from a small country town, she turned sulky. She abandoned the makeup and flopped into a chair to flip through a magazine. Jane coaxed and cajoled, flattered and fussed, but trying to get Mia moving was like herding cats.

Jane was calling Rafe on her mobile to ask him to come up, when Cole knocked on the door. Mia blinked up at the tall, elegantly masculine figure and instantly transformed into her favorite role—seductress. Her dressing gown magically loosened, partially exposing her lush breasts. She turned on her charisma and beamed a thousand-watt smile in Cole's direction.

"Are you my date?" she cooed as she slid a finger provocatively inside the top of his cummerbund. "Jane, why didn't you tell me your friend was so gorgeous?"

Behind Mia's back, Jane rolled her eyes at Cole. "I wanted to surprise you."

"Mmm, mmm. We are going to have a good time tonight," she purred up at Cole. "Aren't we, sugar?"

"O-kay," Jane said, deciding Mia's act had gone on long enough. "The premiere starts in fifteen minutes. Time to get this show on the road."

"They can't start without *me,* sweetie," Mia said, not even looking at Jane.

"Jane's right, you'd better get dressed," Cole said, gently extricating himself from her entangling arms. "I'll be waiting for you in the limo. With a glass of champagne."

Mia waggled her fingers and fluttered off to the bathroom. Jane shuffled Cole unceremoniously out the door.

"She's not the only one who's pleasurably surprised," Cole murmured to Jane. "Why didn't you tell me Mia Mac-Donald is every schoolboy's wet dream?"

"Don't get any ideas," she said, hurrying

him down the corridor. "No matter what Mia says or does, your job is not hands-on."

"Says who?" Cole caught a glimpse of himself in one of the large gilt mirrors that lined the hallway and automatically started to smooth down his hair.

"Don't *do* that." Jane reached up and tousled it again. Looking up at him, she was bowled over by a surge of exasperated affection. "You look great."

"*Gorgeous,* apparently," he corrected, grinning.

"Stop it or I'll have to smack you."

She hardly spoke to Cole again during the limo ride to the movie theater and the walk down the red carpet. She and Rafe had gone first, leaving Mia to leisurely pose for the cameras while Cole followed in her wake. In the darkened theater she'd glanced over and seen Mia feeding Cole canapés while an usher filled his champagne glass. She doubted Cole had seen more than five consecutive minutes of the movie.

Now, through the smoke haze hanging over their table, she watched the actress drape herself all over Cole and felt like smacking Mia. Cole was lapping it up. Disgusting. He might be having fun but he'd completely forgotten that his goal tonight was to talk to Rafe about buying the Rasmussen estate.

"Cole?" No response. Jane leaned over the table and spoke louder. *"Cole."* He was concentrating so hard on Mia's cleavage that he didn't have enough brainpower left to work his ears. Jane threw a bread roll and hit him on the nose.

"Hey!" he complained, brushing away crumbs.

"Cole, did you know that Mia has a fabulous singing voice?" Jane said. "Mia, why don't you get up and give us a tune from the movie."

"Oh, I don't want to work tonight."

"Rafe would love to hear you sing." Beside her, Rafe made a noise of protest. She kicked him under the table.

Mia rose in a swish of scarlet chiffon. She leaned over the table, using her arms to push her cleavage to greater heights. *"Do* you want to hear me sing, Rafe?"

"If I survived that ghastly red-carpet

walk I suppose I'll live through anything."
Rafe puffed away on a cigarette, paying no
attention to the breasts bubbling out at
him.

Pouting, Mia turned to Cole. "This
one's for *you,* darling."

Then, smiling graciously at the diners
on either side, she sashayed over to the
gleaming black grand piano on the dais
and struck a pose. The piano player,
eyebrows raised, segued into one of the
melodies from *Swept Away.* Mia's sultry
voice rose and the restaurant grew quiet,
everyone listening with rapt attention.

COLE FLASHED a grateful smile across the
table at Jane for gaining him respite from
Mia. Then again, it was the least she could
do after setting him up with that nympho-
egomaniac. Despite what he'd told Jane, he
didn't have the slightest interest in the
actress. But he *was* fascinated by Jane
trying to hide the fact that she was as
jealous as a green-eyed harpy. He was
fairly certain Mia's attention was an
attempt to induce the same feelings in

Rafe, though judging by Rafe's total disregard, that wasn't working so well for her.

The red-carpet walk to the doors of the cinema had been surreal. Photographers' flashbulbs blinding him, he'd plastered a self-conscious smirk on his face and strolled two steps behind Mia like a prince consort behind a queen. Mia had smiled and waved to her loyal subjects, stopping now and then to sign autographs. More than a few women had asked for his autograph and he'd happily obliged, chuckling inwardly when they glanced at his signature with puzzled frowns and realized they didn't know who the hell he was.

His focus kept drifting to Jane, gliding along on Rafe's arm. Jane's understated elegance was vastly more attractive to him than Mia's sexual opulence. But being a celebrity's handbag did have certain advantages. Viewing the film in a cordoned-off section of the theater, a drink in one hand and savory nibbles in the other, had been a blast. A smile flitted over his face at the memory.

Jane scooted around the table to

occupy Mia's spot next to Cole. "You're loving this," she muttered bitterly. "How can you let her maul you like that? You don't even know her."

"I thought you wanted me to be nice to her? I can't help it if I'm devastatingly attractive to women."

"You don't have to…to *respond*."

"I'm a red-blooded male. I could hate her guts and my body would still respond."

"She would drop you at a moment's notice if she saw someone she liked better."

He didn't doubt it. In fact, he was starting to long for that moment. If it didn't come soon enough, *he'd* have to discourage *her*. Although, judging from her obsession with the obviously disinterested Rafe, Cole suspected that ignoring her might only increase her interest in him.

"What are you waiting for?" Jane went on, nodding at Rafe. "Get over there and give him your sales pitch before he passes out from too much champagne."

He glanced across the table. Jane was right; Rafe *was* becoming a tad glassy-eyed. Time to make his move.

"All right, I'm going," he said to Jane. "Wish me luck."

As Mia launched into another song, Cole slid into the chair Jane had vacated next to Rafe. "She has a good voice, doesn't she?"

"Not bad," Rafe acknowledged. "Pity she can't act."

"Does it matter when you look like that?"

Rafe gave him a withering glance. "Jane is worth ten of her, in looks *and* talent."

Cole had only intended to make a little small talk before launching into a discussion of the Red Hill property market, but this comment he couldn't let pass. "I agree completely. She was a huge hit in our high school production. Surprised the hell out of everyone."

"It doesn't surprise me." Rafe lit a cigarette. "No one will ever know how far she could have gone."

"So why did she give up acting?"

Rafe glanced at him through curling blue smoke. "She gave it up when Mary Kate developed asthma."

Cole found a glass of water that hadn't been touched and took a drink. "She mentioned that, but how did that affect her career?"

"Her career was starting to take off just about the time Mary Kate's asthma kicked in. The doctors ruled out physical causes and concluded it was an emotional response to Jane being gone a lot."

"Filming, you mean?" Cole asked.

"Right. When Jane got the lead in a movie being filmed in Hawaii, deep in the jungle, it meant leaving Mary Kate with a nanny for weeks at a time."

"Jane wouldn't have liked that," Cole murmured.

"No, she was hesitant, but in the end she took the role. She'd been gone a week when the girl had a severe attack and was rushed to hospital. She survived but Jane pulled out of the film." Rafe shrugged, a drink in one hand, a cigarette in the other. "She got a reputation for being unreliable. That was the end of her acting career."

"I wonder why she didn't tell me that," Cole said, glancing across the table to where Jane was chatting to the woman on her right, a screenwriter. "Why did she pretend it was because her acting wasn't good enough?"

"She doesn't tell anyone," Rafe said. "Maybe she doesn't want Mary Kate to feel guilty because her mother didn't get to do what she loved. Maybe she wants to forget she ever had those ambitions. Who knows? I only told you because you're Mary Kate's father." Rafe jabbed the glowing end of his cigarette at Cole. "You'd better not blow Jane's secret to the girl."

"I won't." Cole applauded with the rest of the audience as Mia finished her song. He saw her thank the piano player then bow to the audience. "My date is on her way back so I'd better cut to the chase. I understand you're interested in property in Red Hill."

Rafe stubbed out his cigarette. All at once he looked alert and sober. "Tell me about the estate. Jane says it's got a six-car garage. I've got a collection of vintage Mustangs."

Cole gave him a low-key sales pitch, quickly highlighting the many features of the estate. "You have to see this place to appreciate it." He took a business card from his wallet and handed it to Rafe. "Come out next week and have a look. I'd be happy to show you around anytime."

He rose as Jane came to reclaim her seat, giving her a discreet thumbs-up.

SHORTLY AFTER 3:00 a.m. Jane trailed barefoot through the deserted hotel lobby, her ivory high heels dangling from her fingers. Music and laughter filtered through from the bar.

Cole had talked to Rafe for all of six minutes. Then Mia had returned triumphantly from the dais and monopolized him for the rest of the evening. The last Jane had seen of them, they'd been getting into a chauffeured limo outside the restaurant. If he wanted to spend the night with Mia, fine. No, not fine. She didn't want Cole, but neither did she want him to want Mia. Which made no sense, but it was late and she was too tired to be rational.

After the party in the restaurant, Rafe had dragged her to the casino where she'd watched him throw away a small fortune on the roulette wheel. She'd placed small cautious bets then allowed the spinning black-and-red blur to stop her from thinking about Cole and Mia together.

"Feel like a nightcap?"

Jane froze then slowly turned. Cole was sitting in a high-backed chair facing the row of lifts. "What are *you* doing here? I thought you'd be with Mia."

Then she noticed that his hair had gone from stylishly tousled to bed-head messy and his bow tie dangled loose around his neck. "Or have you come and gone?"

"Not that it's any of your business but I respect myself too much to sleep with a woman on the first date."

"Yeah, right." Jane's heart did a little dance. *He hadn't slept with Mia.*

"She's not my type," Cole went on. "Besides, you're a much better kisser."

"Wait a minute… You *kissed* her?"

"Just a small kiss. Just a touch. Nothing, really."

"Nothing? Then I suppose you'd call our kiss the other night nothing, too."

"*You* were the one who said that it was

nothing. *I* didn't think so. *I* thought it was something." Cole unfolded himself from the chair and rose. "You didn't answer my question. A nightcap?"

"I don't know," she replied, still miffed.

"One drink won't hurt." Cole put his arm lightly around her shoulders and steered her toward the bar. "What have *you* been up to?"

She lifted the beaded ivory purse that weighed a ton and jingled the coins inside. "Playing roulette. I saw Joey in the casino lobby."

Cole groaned. "Not again. Did you speak to him?"

"No, I was too busy." She grinned and cradled her bulging purse. "I won three hundred dollars."

"In that case, I'll set aside my objections to gambling for one night," Cole said. "You're buying."

She ordered the drinks and they found a table in a quiet corner. Jane sipped her Kahlúa and cream. "Remember drinking this in high school?"

"It's a stroll down memory lane, all

right." Cole grimaced. "I can't believe you talked me into it."

"You're very suggestible." She grinned over the top of her glass. "Admit it, you love it."

"I admit nothing." He took another sip and eyed her thoughtfully. "Tonight has convinced me I could never work with movie stars. Good thing you had no talent or you could have become like Mia."

Jane didn't allow herself to react to Cole's teasing. "Mia's just doing what people expect of her. She's actually pretty smart. Rafe pretends to be a shambling drunk but he's incredibly sharp. You can't be a good actor without a certain level of intelligence."

"Yes, I can see that." He eyed her narrowly. "Sometimes you wouldn't even know they're acting."

Jane swirled her drink. "What exactly did you and Rafe talk about tonight?"

Cole leaned forward. "Why didn't you tell me you quit acting because of Mary Kate's asthma?"

Very calmly, she said, "I'm going to kill Rafe."

"I dragged it out of him. Seriously, why not tell me?"

"I don't want any pity. And I don't want Mary Kate to know. So forget it because I have." She sipped her drink. "In all the excitement tonight I forgot to tell you the vendor accepted my latest offer for the apartment. And no Cherry Magoo tried to top me."

"Congratulations." He touched his glass to hers. "My term deposit has come out and is in my account. First thing Monday morning I'll write you a check for the farm."

"Perfect. Then I can put down my deposit." Jane drained her glass. "Speaking of property sales, how did it go with Rafe? I asked him if you two had arranged something but his focus was on the roulette ball and I couldn't tell if his grunt was affirmative or negative."

"Affirmative." Cole's smile turned smug. "He's coming out this week to view the Rasmussen estate."

"That's wonderful. If anyone can afford it, he can." She glimpsed his watch upside down and was shocked to see it was nearly 4:00 a.m. "I'd better go up. It's really late."

"Or really early." He slid his hand over her wrist and rested his thumb lightly on her pulse point. "We could go to my room."

Cole's smoky gaze held her, the soft music lulled her, the Kahlúa warmed her blood. The thought of falling into bed with him was far too appealing. Jane pulled her hand away and rose. "Thanks for coming tonight. I know it was a real hardship."

"Don't hide behind sarcasm," Cole said. "Admit it, you and I have got chemistry happening."

"I don't know what you're talking about." She started to walk away.

"I'm talking about how jealous you were tonight of me and Mia."

"Oh, you are so arrogant." Jane sat down again abruptly. "I was *not* jealous."

"Then why were you looking daggers at her all evening?"

"She annoys me the way she uses her sexuality to get what she wants. Now *you're* annoying me, acting like I've got a…a schoolgirl crush on you. Trust me, that was over long ago."

Cole leaned forward, his voice low and urgent. "How can it be a schoolgirl crush when you're every inch a woman? I want you, too. Can't you tell?"

Heat flooded through her. Jane's breath caught in her throat. "You're wrong," she whispered hoarsely. "I feel nothing for you."

"Can you look me in the eye and deny there's an attraction between us?" he demanded.

"Maybe there's a physical one." Seizing upon the distinction, she made her voice firmer. "But this *thing* between us isn't emotional. You killed my love thirteen years ago. I thought I had made love to someone who loved me. But I was wrong, and now *I* respect myself too much to sleep with a man who lied to me, who said he loved me when he didn't."

The fire faded suddenly from Cole's eyes. His jaw tightened and he leaned back. "That was a long time ago. This is now."

"For a man who prides himself on his

honesty you sure told a whopper that time." Jane got to her feet. "I'm going to bed. Alone. Good night, Cole."

She walked out of the bar without a backward glance.

Cole waited until she'd gone through the door. Then he buried his face in his hands. If she only knew why he put such a premium on honesty these days. Thirteen years ago he'd told a whopper all right. He'd told her he didn't love her. And he'd been suffering the consequences of that lie ever since.

CHAPTER TWELVE

"DID YOU AND MOM have a good time at the premiere?" Mary Kate had only listened with half an ear to Cole's instructions on how to answer the office phone, concentrating instead on trying to gauge from his manner whether the weekend had left her parents softer toward each other or unchanged.

"The movie was excellent, the dinner was delicious, the company was entertaining. Now, can you repeat back to me what I just said?"

"The movie was excellent—"

"You know what I meant," Cole cut in. "And you're in no position to be cheeky, my girl. You're still being punished. While Millie's at lunch, you and Stephanie might have to actually run the office if Joey and I need to go out."

"I'm sorry," she said meekly. "I'm to sit at the desk and answer the phone." In a musical voice, she demonstrated. "'Good morning, this is Red Hill Real Estate, Mary Kate speaking. May I help you?' If you're not here I take a message and if you are, I say, 'One moment, please,' and press the white button on the phone to put the call through."

"Very good." Cole sounded relieved. "Stephanie, what are you doing?"

Stephanie drew herself up, arms stiff by her sides. "Yes, sir. I'm to sort the contents of the beige tray alphabetically into folders in the gray cabinet. Sir."

"At ease," he said dryly. "This isn't a military prison. When you've done the filing you can water the plants."

"Then what?" Stephanie asked. "Sir."

"Then I'll think of something else." He started back to his office then noticed she was still standing to attention. "Cut it out."

"Yes, sir." Stephanie saluted and relaxed.

"Stop saying sir."

"Yes, sir!"

Shaking his head like a man besieged, Cole escaped back into his office and shut the door.

Mary Kate made a dash for the chair behind the desk. She bounced into it and gripped the arms, reveling in her power. "This is going to be so cool. It's like a real job and I'm in control of this whole office."

"It's not fair that you get to be the receptionist," Stephanie grumbled as she picked up the overflowing tray. "I'm the oldest."

"Only by a month," Mary Kate reminded her. The phone rang. She stared at it. It rang again.

"Answer it," Stephanie urged.

Cole stepped out of his office, eyebrows raised. Mary Kate wiped a palm on her shorts and picked up the receiver. "Hello? I mean, can I help you? Red Hill Real Estate." To her horror, she finished with a squeaky plea. "Do you want to speak to Cole?" She pushed the white button to transfer the call. Cole picked up and Mary Kate relaxed. "I thought I handled that pretty well."

"Talking on the phone is nothing compared to making sure important papers go in the right place." Stephanie had the top drawer of the cabinet open and was placing manila files into alphabetized hanging folders.

Mary Kate swiveled back and forth, frowning. "Time is running out. Cole was just as button-lipped as Mom about what happened when they stayed over-night in the city."

"Nothing happened," Stephanie said flatly. "We need to go to plan B. Have you thought of it yet?"

Mary Kate shook her head. "Mom is depositing Cole's check this morning. It doesn't look like we're going to be able to stop the money from being transferred to her account. Once it is, her check to Jason can be cleared. Bingo, she's got the apart-ment in the bag."

"Unless," Stephanie said slowly, "we hack into Dad's account and move the money somewhere else before it can get sent to your mum's account."

Mary Kate dismissed that with a flap of

her hand. "We'd need his password and account number, and the password and number of another account to move it to."

Stephanie glanced down at the open file. A slow grin spread over her face. "Guess what I've got in my hands?"

"Get out!" Mary Kate jumped up and ran over to look. Sure enough, there were the payroll bank statements and on a separate sheet there was a list of neatly typed account passwords. "Honest people are too trusting. Cole's going to have to beef up security around here. After we're done, that is."

Stephanie chewed on her lip, a worried frown taking over her face. "Dad notices if I take a couple of dollars for lunch money from the brass bowl full of change on top of his dresser. When he finds out about the missing deposit money, we'll never ride horses again as long as we live."

"He won't think it's us, silly. Remember why Wicked Uncle Joey got fired?" Mary Kate argued. "We'll transfer the money from Cole's account into Joey's."

"Oh my God, Mary Kate," Stephanie

exclaimed in a shocked whisper. "You're brilliant! But it's a crime. It's not very nice to Uncle Joey, either."

"Later, we'll admit we did it, not him. Anyway, we're not going to *keep* the money," Mary Kate explained. "We're simply moving it to another location temporarily. Banks do this sort of thing all the time, according to Mom. Think of the big picture. You and me, my mom and our dad, together as a family. Isn't that worth a risk?"

Stephanie gazed at her in awe. "You're *so* bad."

"You're badder."

"Am not."

"Are too."

"You thought of it."

"You're going along with it."

Stephanie stuck her tongue out. Mary Kate did it back. Then they both collapsed in giggles.

Cole's door opened. Stephanie leaped across the room to the filing cabinet and hastily shoved the file in the hanging folder. Mary Kate folded her hands on the desk and tried to look innocent.

Cole emerged, putting on his suit jacket. "I've got to show a client a couple of houses. Will you two be okay for an hour?"

"Sure." Mary Kate exchanged a glance with Stephanie. "We'll be fine."

"No trouble now." Cole tucked his listings book under his arm. "If anyone comes in, get their name and contact details and tell them I'll get back to them later today."

"Okay, Daddy," Stephanie said. "Sir."

He threw her a narrow-eyed glance, then exited, trying to stifle a chuckle.

Mary Kate waited until she saw his car go past up the street then booted up the computer. "Where's that file, Stephanie? Let's hustle."

LATER THAT WEEK, Cole was punching figures into his calculator and muttering to himself. "Ten thousand grafted rootstock at roughly five dollars each, that's fifty thousand…plus delivery…plus labor."

He leaned back, tapping his pen on the pad of paper, as he studied the columns of figures. Start-up expenses would amount to over a hundred thousand dollars. Getting the commission from the Rasmussen estate sale was going to be essential. He'd expected Rafe to call for an appointment by now but actors probably didn't keep normal business hours.

The bell over the entrance door rang. A second later Jane was banging open his door. He hadn't seen her since the morning after the premiere. "Good morning."

"We have a problem." Jane pulled a slip of paper from her purse and threw it on his desk. "Jason called me this morning. My deposit check bounced. The reason was, *your* check didn't clear."

"It's been five days. It shouldn't take that long. I'll call my bank manager."

"You do that. But it's not because the bank is slow. There were insufficient funds in your account."

"Impossible. I saw the amount entered in my online account on my computer." Frowning, Cole reached for the phone and stabbed out his banker's number. "We'll sort this out right away, don't worry."

"A young professional couple is interested in buying the apartment, too," Jane fretted. "They're real, I ran into them at Jason's office. They're waiting to hear about financing, a mere formality apparently, and as soon as they do, they'll be signing on the dotted line."

Cole listened to what she was saying. Then Gordon Bennett came on the line and he sat up straight. "Hey, Gordo. How's it going? I've got a little problem. A check I wrote didn't clear. There must be some mix-up because I *know* I had enough in that account. No, not the trust account for Red Hill Real Estate. My personal checking account. Remember I liquidated a term deposit for a private real estate deal? Yes, one hundred thousand. Sure, I'll hang on."

Cole rested the receiver on his shoulder and smiled reassuringly at Jane. "He's looking into it. This will all be cleared up in a few minutes. Must be a clerical error."

Jane smiled uneasily, her brow still creased in a frown. "I have a bad feeling about this."

"Hello? Yes, I'm here," Cole said into

the phone. Gord's terse recital of the facts sent his stomach into free fall. "You can't just lose a hundred thousand dollars. Where *is* it?" Unable to sit, Cole got to his feet. "What do you mean, you have no idea? The money was removed from my account. It had to be someone from your bank— "Unless…" He fell abruptly back to his chair. Taking a deep breath, he attempted to speak in an even voice. "Gord, I just thought of something. My brother has an account with your bank, too. Is it possible the money was mistakenly transferred to his account?"

Cole heard a sharp intake of breath. Jane's jaw had clamped tight. He tapped his fingers on his desk. "Relax, Jane. I'm sure it's just a mistake. A bank error."

"Mistake, my eye!" Jane hissed. "Joey's taken money before. Don't forget he was in the casino Saturday night."

"Circumstantial evidence," Cole insisted. Though he had to admit, it looked bad. "Joey promised me he wouldn't do anything like that again."

"And you believed him? Isn't it

obvious? He stole it, then he gambled it away!"

Cole shifted in his chair so he could plant both elbows on the desk. "C'mon, Gord. What's taking you so long?"

The bank manager came back on the line and relayed his findings.

"I see. Right. Well, move the money back to my account. No, *I'll* talk to my brother first. If I'm not satisfied, I'll call you in." Cole hung up and tugged his tie loose. God, he hated the noose. When he had his own vineyard he'd never wear one again. "The money did somehow get into Joey's account," he said to Jane. "The good news is, he didn't gamble and lose it."

"Great. All he did was steal it. I can't believe you still defend him." She threw her hands in the air. "Where *is* Joey? Aren't you going to call him and ask for an explanation?"

"Of course." Cole reached for his mobile and punched a number in the speed dial. Joey's mobile was shut off. "I forgot. Joey has today off. He and Crystal were going to a movie."

Jane groaned. "Meanwhile, my apartment is going to be sold because I can't come up with the deposit."

"I'll write you out another check immediately." Cole got his checkbook out of the drawer and reached for his pen. "I don't know how this happened but I'm positive Joey didn't steal the money. He promised—"

"Don't!" She rose, holding her hands up to stop him. "If I hear you defend that brother of yours one more time, I'll scream."

"What do you mean, 'that brother of mine'?" Cole rose, too. "Joey's a little immature but he's good-hearted—"

"You're doing it again." She pointed a finger at Cole and started backing out of his office.

"But—"

"*Stop.*"

"Joey's—"

"I mean it, I'm going to scream."

"Calm down. It's only an apartment. There'll be another one around the corner. There always is."

"That's easy for you to say. What if you

lost your bid on the farm because some idiot took your money?"

"Are you calling my brother an idiot?" he asked.

"If the dunce cap fits." Grim-faced, Jane turned her back on him and strode out the door.

"The situation is completely different," he called after her. "The farm is my family's *home*. Hey, don't you walk away from me!"

JANE'S CAR SPUN out on the gravel that littered the entrance to the small shopping strip where Cole's office was located. Damn hick town. They couldn't even keep the street free of dirt.

She roared off up the road, the Mazda's engine growling. Why was Cole so blind about his brother? Blind and stupid and trusting. And a liar. Don't forget that! Her foot pressed harder on the accelerator at the thought, and she fishtailed across the white line as she drove fast around the corner.

Somehow Jane made it home without crashing the car. Coming up the driveway, she saw Cherry and Magoo tethered in the side yard and slowed to avoid spooking them.

She ran up the steps and into the house to the sound of Mary Kate and Stephanie giggling in the kitchen. Those girls had better not be making a mess. She was so angry she was likely to bite their heads off for the slightest infraction. Venting her fury and frustration, she kicked an empty cardboard box out of the entryway to the lounge room.

Mary Kate appeared around the corner, eyes wide. "What's wrong?"

"Joey," she said tersely. "He took money out of Cole's account and Cole's check to me bounced. I'll probably lose the apartment because of him." She threw her hands in the air. "And Cole's defending him! We had a huge fight." She slumped onto the couch, suddenly drained of energy.

Stephanie came out of the kitchen to stand at Mary Kate's side. She nudged Mary Kate. Mary Kate frowned.

"Hi, Stephanie," Jane said listlessly. She

glanced from one girl to the other. "What's up with you two?"

Mary Kate stepped forward. "Uh, Mom? There's something we'd better tell you. It wasn't Joey who moved that money."

COLE DROVE to Joey's house after work. It was a long shot since Joey still wasn't answering his phone but knowing his brother, he'd simply forgotten to turn it back on. Sure enough, the lights were on in the small cottage his brother and Crystal rented, scattered like others of its kind, among tall trees to the north of the town center.

No one answered Cole's knock. He tried again. Nothing. Yet he could hear faint noises inside, something like voices but without words. Turning the handle, he discovered the door was unlocked.

"Joey?" he called and stepped inside.

The muffled sounds were coming from the back of the house. He walked past the bedroom, down the hall, into the kitchen. The voices grew louder. Joey and Crystal were definitely in the house. "Joey?"

No answer. He listened more closely.

Ah, the laundry room. That was odd, he thought as he pushed open the door. It almost sounded as though they were—

"Joey?" Cole's jaw dropped.

"Dude!" His brother's aggrieved face appeared over Crystal's bare shoulder. The half-naked pair were sprawled in a pile of laundry wedged between the washing machine and the sink. A pair of jockey shorts adorned Joey's head. Crystal's face turned bright red and she grabbed for a towel to cover herself.

"Oh, God. Sorry, Crystal." Cole shut the door quickly.

He was pacing the lounge room when Joey appeared a few minutes later fully dressed with the underwear presumably back where it belonged.

"You should knock before you barge in," Joey said, buttoning his shirt.

"I'm sorry. You should lock your door when you do stuff like that." Cole shook his head. "The *laundry* room?"

"Hey, wherever, you know?" Joey grinned and flopped into the nearest chair. "What's up?"

Cole moved aside a stack of car magazines and sat opposite Joey on the couch. Before he could begin, his mobile phone rang. Frowning, he clicked it directly onto message bank without even checking who was calling. He didn't want any interruptions. Turning his attention back to Joey, he said, "I'm going to ask you something and you have to be completely honest with me. No mucking around, Joey. This is serious. Promise me you'll tell me the truth?"

Joey sat up straight and pushed a hand through his hair. "Yeah, sure."

"I mean it," Cole said. "If you have anything to do with this, I won't be able to cover for you. I won't want to. We're talking jail terms here."

"Dude! I didn't do anything. What's this about?"

Cole took a deep breath. He looked straight into Joey's eyes. "Did you move a hundred thousand dollars from my bank account into yours?"

"A hundred grand. No way!"

"You're sure?"

"I think I'd remember something like that. Besides, I'm skint."

"Jane said she saw you in the casino on Saturday night. Were you gambling?"

"Crystal and I went to dinner there. I played the slots for maybe half an hour." Joey held up two fingers. "Scout's honor."

"You were never a Boy Scout." Cole gripped his knees, the desire to believe Joey warring with the fear that his brother was headed for trouble. He decided it was long past time Joey knew the truth about their father. "Do you know how Dad died?"

"He lost control of the car and ran into a tree." Joey made an impatient gesture. "What's that got to do with me?"

"It wasn't an accident," Cole said quietly.

"What are you saying?" Joey leaned forward, frowning. "I don't understand."

"He had huge gambling debts he couldn't pay. He was about to lose the farm, his standing in the community, quite possibly his family."

It took a minute for the implications to sink in.

"Oh, God." Joey turned white. "No one ever told me."

"You were only nine. Mum didn't want you to know."

Joey dropped his face in his hands. His shoulders lifted and fell. Cole was about to go to him, when Crystal came out of the kitchen and stood behind Joey's chair. Her brown curls were ruffled and the collar of her pink blouse was stuck up on one side. She began to knead Joey's shoulders.

"What's going on?" she asked. "If it's about the casino, Joey only played the slots for a little while then we went to a show. Honest. He was the one to call it quits." She leaned over and kissed his cheek. "I'm so proud of you."

"Babe, I'm never going again, not even for half an hour," Joey said fervently.

"This isn't about the casino," Cole said. "Though I'm glad to hear Joey's exercising control." He explained briefly about the money being transferred from his account to Joey's. Again, he asked, "Do you swear you know nothing about it?"

Joey dragged his hands down his face.

His eyes were moist, his voice ragged. "I swear. That's the truth. I know I joke around, but I meant it when I made you that promise. You're my brother. You gave me another chance, I'm not about to go back on my word."

Cole flexed his fingers, letting them relax. "I believe you."

Joey nodded limply. "Okay, then. You know, I'm not a kid anymore. You should have told me about Dad before now."

Cole rose and clasped him by the shoulder. "Mum wanted to preserve his memory for you. But you're right." He stepped back. "I've got to go. Sorry to disturb you both. Really sorry about that, Crystal."

She smiled, embarrassed. "Just wipe that image from your mind, okay?"

Cole had far more troubling things on his mind as he drove home. *If Joey hadn't moved the money, then who the hell had?*

Idling at an intersection while a truck went by, he remembered the call to his mobile and retrieved the message. It was

Jane, her voice high and tight. "Get over here *right away*. The girls have really done it this time."

THE GIRLS SAT side by side on the couch, holding hands. Stephanie hung her head. Mary Kate held hers high, two spots of color in her cheeks as she stared straight ahead. Jane paced the lounge room while Cole ranted and raved.

"How on earth could you commit such a knuckle-brained, idiotic prank?" He scowled at Stephanie and Mary Kate. "You'll both be lucky if you don't end up in juvy."

"What's juvy?" Stephanie whispered to Mary Kate.

"A place for juvenile delinquents," Mary Kate replied.

"I *trusted* you girls," he went on. "You had access to confidential files. How could you let me down like this? How could you sabotage Jane? You two have been trying to stop her from leaving Red Hill since she got here."

"You want her to stay, too, don't you?" Stephanie asked diffidently.

Cole stared at her. "My feelings on the matter are irrelevant."

"We did if for you," Mary Kate spoke up. She turned to her mother. "And you, Mom. We wanted to stop you from buying the apartment so you and Cole could have time to fall in love. And it worked. Well, part of it."

"Just which part did you think worked?" Jane demanded. "You and I will *not* be living in Red Hill. And there isn't time enough on earth for Cole and me to fall in love with each other."

Cole whipped his head around. She glared back at him.

Then she returned her attention to Stephanie and Mary Kate. "There will be no more contact between you two. No riding, no telephone, no e-mail. Nothing."

"For how long?" both girls wailed.

"Until we say differently," Cole answered.

"You will apologize to Cole," Jane added with anextrasevere glance at Mary Kate. "And Joey, in writing."

"I'm sorry." At last Mary Kate dropped her head in contrition. "We didn't mean any harm. Honest. We couldn't have let Joey take the blame."

"I'm sorry, too." Tears ran down Stephanie's cheeks. "We just wanted us all to be t-together."

"We wanted you both to be happy," Mary Kate added miserably.

"All right, that's enough," Cole said gruffly, putting a hand on Stephanie's shoulder. "Let's get going."

At the door, Stephanie ran back to Mary Kate. Sobbing, the pair embraced as if going to their doom. Jane met Cole's gaze over their heads and shrugged helplessly. She was still angry, the girls should have known better, but she believed their motives had been sincere. Cole rolled his eyes as if in silent agreement. For the first time in this sorry episode Jane felt as if she could manage a small smile. In a way the girls hadn't intended, they *had* brought Cole and Jane together.

Stephanie tore away and ran outside. Mary Kate, still crying, ran upstairs.

Jane walked Cole out to the veranda.

She touched his shoulder then quickly drew her hand away. "I'm sorry, too. About all those things I said about Joey. I was wrong."

"Never mind," Cole said wearily. "Just promise me we'll keep up their punishment for at least a week." He rubbed the back of his neck, rolled his shoulders.

"You're working too hard," Jane noted sympathetically.

"I don't mind the hard work but the pressure gets to me," Cole admitted.

"Has Rafe called you?"

"Not yet. I left a message with him yesterday but he hasn't gotten back to me." Cole's mouth drew down. "Maybe he's changed his mind."

"He's probably just busy. I'll contact him and jog his memory."

"Thanks." Cole took out his wallet and removed a check written out for the deposit. He handed it to her. "You left in rather a hurry earlier. The money's in my account. My bank manager said he'll watch out for the check and process it immediately. His number is on the back if your Realtor wants to call him. If you get that in right away, you should be okay."

Jane glanced at her watch. "If I leave now I can just make it."

Cole squeezed her hand. "Good luck."

He walked back to his car. Jane leaned against the door frame and watched until his Porsche had bumped down the potholed driveway and disappeared below the crest of the hill. Then she stirred herself. There was no time to waste.

CHAPTER THIRTEEN

"MARY KATE?" JANE CALLED as she ran upstairs. There was no answer. She found her daughter tucked up in bed, her face buried in her pillow. Touching her shoulder, Jane repeated, "Mary Kate."

The girl rolled onto her back. Her eyes were red and her cheeks tearsstained. At the sight of her mother, fresh moisture welled in her eyes. "Are you going to lose the apartment?"

"I hope not," Jane said. "I'm driving into Melbourne now to hand over the deposit. I was going to suggest you come but you'd better stay here, after all."

Sniffing, Mary Kate nodded. "I'll be good."

Jane kissed her forehead. "See you later."

She arrived at the city realty office just

before closing. The receptionist was on the phone so Jane bypassed the front desk and went straight to Jason's office.

As the young man was hanging up the phone, he said, "That was the couple who are interested in the apartment. Their finance has been approved and they're coming in first thing in the morning."

"Well, I'm here now." Jane plunked the check down on his desk. "I can guarantee this will clear without delay."

"In that case—" Jason smiled and held out his hand "—congratulations."

Jane shook, blinking back tears of relief. "Wonderful. Thank you so very much."

Her mind whirled all the way home in the car—Cole, the move, Mary Kate and Stephanie—so much was happening, so many things to think about. She was so preoccupied she missed her turnoff from the freeway onto Red Hill Road and drove miles past before she could make an exit.

Stopped at a crossroads, she peered through the windscreen at the street signs and chewed her lip, wondering which road to take. Then she noticed a small billboard on the shoulder, pointing the way to the Rye Hot Springs Spa. The color picture of steaming hot pools made her conscious of the tension in her shoulders and neck. On impulse she put on her indicator and made the turn.

Of course she wouldn't go in now—she didn't have her bathing suit with her and she wanted to get back to Mary Kate, but there was no harm in checking it out. The young woman behind the desk, a tall sleek blonde, let her walk through and view the pools. Some were public, some private; they were even more enticing than she'd expected.

"I'll come back tomorrow," Jane told the woman as another impulse struck her. "Book me a private pool in the evening."

"I'm sorry," the woman said, scanning the appointment book. "We have no evenings available all week. I can give you Wednesday next week."

Who knew where she'd be next week? "I'd like something sooner."

"Three o'clock tomorrow?"

Jane nodded. "That'll have to do."

The attendant filled in a card with the time and date reserved for the private pool. She put it in an envelope and handed it to Jane.

"Thanks," Jane said. "Now, can you tell me how to get to Red Hill from here?"

Twenty minutes later Jane drove into town from a back road. Most of the shops had shut except for the grocery store and the pharmacy. Red Hill Real Estate was closed, as she'd expected. So she wrote Cole's name on the envelope and slipped it through the mail slot in the door.

Giddy, she hurried back to her car. All she could think of now was tomorrow.

COLE GLANCED AT HIS WATCH—nearly two-thirty. The small square envelope lay on his desk. Across the crisp white paper Jane had written, *Hope you can make it.*

He still hadn't heard from Rafe Baldwyn. Frankly, he was getting a little nervous. He'd taken a huge risk in purchasing Cockatoo Ridge. Picking up his pen, he began to tap it against the blotter.

Stephanie poked her head in his office.

"I've finished dusting the Venetian blinds. What do you want me to do now?"

Cole searched his brain for another boring, innocuous job. "Check the house pictures in the window and if any are coming unstuck, put fresh tape on them."

Stephanie's shoulders slumped as she nodded dispiritedly. Turning to leave, she noticed his ceaseless tapping and paused. "I'm sorry if I make you tense, Daddy."

Cole sighed. "It's not just you, sweetheart. Don't worry."

She nodded at the spa card with the photo of steaming hot pools among fern grottos. "You should go."

He had to admit, it was tempting. He frequently recommended the hot springs to clients but he'd never been there himself. Maybe it was time he found out what all the fuss was about. And Jane would be there.

"I'm waiting for a phone call from Rafe Baldwyn."

"Did he say he was going to call today?" Stephanie asked.

"Well, no," Cole admitted.

"Tell Millie to make him a late appointment if he does ring. That will give you time to get back here."

Cole pursed his lips, unconsciously tugging on his collar. When he noticed what he was doing, he sighed. "You're right. I need to relax." He rose and started unknotting his tie. "But you are not to go into the filing cabinet or go on the computer, understand?"

"Yes," Stephanie said meekly. "I'll be good."

JANE STEPPED INTO the steaming pool and slowly lowered herself until her shoulders were completely submerged. *Ahhhhh.* This was good. *Would Cole accept her invitation?*

Now that the apartment purchase was back on track, she felt she could finally relax. Leaning against the smoothly rounded stone, she surveyed the private pool. It was enclosed on three sides with a brush fence and landscaped with small boulders and colorful grasses. A rock wall rose on the fourth side where ferns overhung the pool and the geothermally heated mineral water spilled from a crevice. A wooden lounge chair with puffy green-and-white cushions offered a restful place out of the water.

This would be her last opportunity for an afternoon like this. The vendor had agreed to a thirty-day settlement and had also agreed to rent her the apartment until settlement went through. She and Mary Kate could be moving in by next weekend.

Jane turned onto her stomach, resting her arms on the edge of the pool with her legs floating out behind her. She watched an ant crawl up the innermost blade in a clump of red flax grass, moving along an invisible path on some important errand.

Where was Cole? Setting up this rendezvous was probably a monumental mistake. But she couldn't stop thinking about him, how good they'd once been together. She wished in some ways they could obliterate their past, and she could act upon her attraction with only the future to think of. But eliminating the past would mean no Mary Kate and that was unthinkable.

The door in the brush fence swung inward. Bare feet walked into her line of vision. She looked up, *waaay* up, past shins dusted with dark brown hair, past sculpted thighs, past blue board shorts, past a broad muscled chest...straight into a pair of green eyes with gold flecks.

"Cole." Even though she'd expected him, her heart gave a little lurch.

"We have to stop meeting like this." Cole walked down two shallow steps and into the water. He sank to his shoulders. Steam beaded on his eyelashes and strands of his hair.

"And yet here we are." Jane pressed herself against the far wall. Damn. This was going to be awkward. In the silence that followed she tried to meditate on the ways of the ant only to quickly give up with a gusty sigh. With her heart beating a mile a minute, achieving serenity was too much of a struggle.

Cole lay back, eyes shut, his head resting against the stone wall, looking far too sexy. Her hand ached to stroke his jaw and discover if his light beard was as soft as it had seemed the night of the premiere. She stopped herself, appalled. How could she feel this way about a man who'd broken her heart? What had she been thinking, inviting him here? Look at him, ignoring her. She might as well be alone in the pool.

"Just so we're clear, I invited you here to apologize for flying off the handle the other day," Jane said primly. "And I want to thank you for fixing things with the bank so quickly."

"You mean, you didn't ask me here for our own pleasure?" Cole asked lazily, opening one eye.

Jane's cheeks burned. "Well, of course, the hot springs are a great way to relax. We've both been working too hard, getting stressed out…"

Cole waded chest-deep across the pool to her. Steam rose around them. The water temperature seemed to climb by several degrees.

"You mean we're not here to kiss…" He brushed his lips across hers so lightly they tingled. "Touch…" His fingers skimmed her cheek before tucking a lock of damp hair behind her ear. "Make love…"

Jane lunged beneath his arm and came up on the other side of the pool. "No, we're not," she said. "The girls tried to put us in romantic situations and expected us to fall into each other's arms as if we were teenagers. But we're—"

"Adults," Cole agreed, lazily watching her. "With adult needs." His biceps and shoulders, spread along the pool's edge, looked as carved as the rock they rested on.

"That's not quite what I meant." Jane blew a wisp of hair out of her eyes and tried to concentrate. The steam was cooking her brain. "We were together such a long time ago, it would be crazy to think we could feel that again."

"You can't step into the same hot pool twice," he pronounced sagely.

"Exactly." Relaxing now that she knew he understood, she let her legs float out.

Below the water, a hand clamped around her ankle. She stifled a gasp. Cole pulled and she was drawn through the pool toward him. Resistance proved as thrilling as it was futile.

"Remember how you wondered if I still

kissed the same way?" His other hand reached for her waist. But it was his eyes that held her. "I've been wondering if you still make those soft moans during love-making."

"I…" Wriggling, she slipped out of his grasp. Then took the offensive and pushed on his chest until he was jammed against the rocks. Talking about sex was almost as hot as the act itself. Dangerously so. "I'm still mad at you for dumping me thirteen years ago."

All she wanted was a crumb, an admission that he had loved her once. She could forgive him for marrying Leslie—after all, he'd asked the other woman first before he'd known Jane was pregnant. But she couldn't forgive him for denying he'd ever loved her.

"Don't be mad. I've suffered, too." He pulled her back into his arms and kissed her. His lips were firm, his arms around her strong. Everything else was pure heat— the water, the air, their skin pressed together.

"No," she said, fighting for breath. To her horror, the moisture in her eyes wasn't from the hot pool. "You lied to me. You told me you loved me. I guess you *have* to tell a seventeen-year-old girl that to get her into bed. When Leslie came home, you went right back to her."

"I didn't want to. Our families pressured us. She was pregnant before I even started up with you, though of course I didn't know it."

"I *understand* all that." God, she wanted to scream. Instead, she took out her frustration by lightly thumping his chest with her fist. "I was going to leave, give you up. But you weren't content with that. You had to tell me you didn't love me."

"I lied."

"I *know.* That's what I can't forgive. You made me think you loved me. Then you denied ever loving me. How do think that made me feel?" Jane gulped back a sob. "All I could conclude was that you'd used me as a sexual fill-in for your absent girl-friend."

"That was never the case." Cole was quiet for a moment, then continued in a soft voice. "I lied when I said I *didn't* love you."

Jane froze, her fists still on his chest.

"What do you mean? Why would you say that?"

Taking her wrists, he lowered her arms. "I wanted you to hate me."

"Well, guess what, buddy? You succeeded!"

"Let me explain," he said. "Leslie came back from her holiday and told me she was pregnant. I asked her to marry me, thinking I was doing the right thing. Her family was pushing for that, too."

"Did you love her?" Jane asked quietly.

"Not the way I loved you. If I'd known you were pregnant, then I would never have proposed to Leslie. But once I had, I couldn't go back on my word."

Jane was silent, trying to absorb all he'd told her. "You still haven't told me why you wanted me to hate you."

"Since we had no chance of being together, I thought I'd make you mad instead of sad. That way you'd find it easier to forget me."

"Oh, for God's sake!" Jane whacked him on the shoulder. "Do you have any idea how much grief that caused me?"

"I know it was dumb. But it seemed to make sense at the time. I probably got it off one of those sentimental movies you made me watch."

"Don't blame your stupid ideas on me." Jane wiped her eyes and pushed herself up on a rock ledge.

"Then there was the other thing."

"What other thing?"

"You had grand ambitions, and an even bigger talent. You talked endlessly about getting away from Red Hill, going to acting school, taking on Hollywood. I didn't know how you were going to do it as a single mum, but if anyone could, it would be you. I believed you had what it takes to succeed."

"Well, we'll never know, will we?" Jane rolled her eyes. "Don't you start on at me about wasting my talent. I'm not sorry. Mary Kate came first."

"Don't get all huffy. I think you did the right thing." Cole reached up and turned her face to him. "The point is, I knew *I* wasn't getting out of Red Hill. Even if it wasn't for Leslie, I couldn't leave my mother and little brother. I promised my father before he died I'd look after them. I wanted to make sure you got your chance."

Jane stared at him, shaking her head. "So you told me you didn't love me."

Cole shrugged, then stepped backward and lowered himself in the water.

"Oh, Cole." She launched herself off the ledge and swam on top of him, looping her arms around his neck.

"You're trying to drown me now." He met her gaze with a smile of heartbreaking tenderness.

She kissed him. And they went under.

Cole surged back to the surface, lifting her out of the pool and depositing her onto the side. "Let's get out."

Jane spread her towel out on a lounge chair and lay down, edging over to make room for him. Heat from the thermal pool clung to his skin. Drops of water fell from him onto her breast and rolled inside her bikini top.

"I thought we weren't going to be manipulated by the girls," she said with a sly smile.

"They didn't invite me here today, you did. We're doing this because we want to." Planting his hands on either side of her head, Cole dropped his mouth to hers and took it in a long slow kiss.

God help her, she did want him. She'd spent years dreaming about making love to him. With a little moan, she slid her arms up his chest and around his neck. Cole broke long enough to inhale sharply, burn his gaze into her eyes. Then he began to drop kisses down her neck, across the tops of her breasts and up the other side of her neck. Jane scooted up the chair, trying to get closer. Cole undid the tie on her bikini halter and the fabric slipped down over her bare breasts. His hand explored, caressing and fondling her nipples. Then he dipped his head and sucked on her nipples, gently at first, then harder, until her nerve endings quivered and a slow deep ache spread through her belly.

His skin was almost dry, with only droplets of water to lubricate the movement of her hands over his shoulders, his chest, his flat abdomen. Lower, to the tautly strained fabric of his shorts. Her hand slid over the hardness of his erection then slipped inside his shorts. She heard the sudden intake of his breath, the creak of the chair.

"What if this thing collapses?" Jane whispered.

Cole rocked it experimentally. "Sturdy as a bed." He undid the clasp at the back of her bikini top. He cast it aside then filled his hands with her breasts.

"What if someone comes?" Jane asked.

"We've got thirty minutes left. No one will come." He slipped off his shorts and stood before her wearing nothing but a wicked grin. "Except you and me."

He pulled her to her feet then sat down in front of her, rubbing his hands up and down her legs, down the outside, up the inside to brush his knuckles against the mound between her legs, a little harder with each stroke. On the final downstroke, he pulled her bikini bottoms down to her ankles. Jane felt his tongue against her, in her, and her knees turned to jelly.

Kneeling on the cushioned chair, legs

quivering with the tension of holding herself in this torturous position, she pulled his hands to her breasts and moaned aloud as his fingers tormented her nipples, promising relief but in fact, stoking the ache to greater heights of exquisite pain. She sank slowly onto his lap, rubbing her breasts down his chest, pushing her aching groin down on him. He'd started to penetrate when she froze.

"We have no condoms." By now she was so aroused she almost didn't care, but she was a responsible adult and in control of herself. Just.

"I...have...one...in...my...wallet," he panted between kisses.

"How long has it been there?"

"Since 1994." She pushed back to see if he was being serious. "I'm *kidding*."

"How long?"

"Since you came back to Red Hill."

It gave her quite a thrill to think it might be true. She climbed off him. "Get it. And hurry."

He found his wallet in his shorts pocket. Found the condom. Put it on. All in about twenty seconds flat. Cole reached for Jane and she wrapped a leg around his calf.

"We can't tell the girls about this," she breathed.

"I'm not in the habit of discussing my sex life with my not quite twelve-year-old daughter," Cole replied.

"Neither am I."

"Do you have a sex life?"

She reared back, ready to object. Then shrugged. "Not so much."

"Good. Don't tell me anything more." He didn't want her to have been with anyone since the last time they'd been together. Since they'd been apart for thirteen years that wasn't likely, but if she'd had a string of lovers, he didn't want to know. She was his; she always had been.

He half lay on the lounge chair and pulled her down on top of him, gazing in wonder at her creamy skin, her lovely curves as his hands refreshed their memory of her firm resilient flesh. She was perfect, not too lush, not too skinny. She shut her eyes and moved against him, hands braced on his chest as she edged back to the point where they'd stopped a few minutes ago, with him poised to enter her.

Then, holding her gaze with his, directing her hips with his hands, he pulled her over him. Slowly, carefully, he pushed, filling her, enveloped by her.

The sound of voices outside in the public pool drifted on the breeze, mingling with their ragged breathing. Mineral-scented steam rose off the hot pool, blending with the musk of skin and sex. He'd dreamed of Jane for years after she left. Now this… the fern grotto, sex in the afternoon, the languor of the hot pool, the flashpoint he was building to—it was all the fantasy he could wish for.

Except it wasn't fantasy. Jane, moving over him with a blissful smile on her face, was real. He could capture her small firm breast in his mouth and taste the pebbled nipple, the salty skin. With every breath he smelled the elusive scent of wildflowers. Through half-closed eyes he could see her body moving against his. Hear her sighs and the soft sounds their bodies made together.

Oh, yes, it didn't get any more real than this.

"*Cole.*" She strained against him, moving faster, biting her lip as she tightened around him.

His fingers dug into the skin of her hips as he thrust harder. Her mouth found his. Meshed tongues, grinding teeth, mingled breath. His senses went haywire. He felt her cry as he heard her shudder of release. His ears were ringing, color exploded behind his eyelids. Wildflowers and musk filled his nostrils. He lost himself, found something spiritual, knew ecstasy. Collapsed. Came to with Jane draped limp and moist across his body, her long hair tickling his sides. His arms holding her. *Holding* her. Never let her go. Ever. Again.

MARY KATE SNEEZED. The dust from Aunt Esther's books filled the air with motes that danced in the sunlight slanting through the window. She'd packed six boxes and there were still four shelves to go.

Unfolding her bent legs she rose from the

floor and went to the kitchen for a drink of water. The clock on the new stove said 3:25 p.m. Mom had gone out without saying where, only that she'd be a couple of hours.

Mary Kate picked up the phone. She'd written a letter to Joey but it would take a couple of days for him to get it. Her crime lay heavy on her conscience and she would feel a whole lot better if she just spoke to him. She dialed the real estate office, her fingers crossed that Millie or Joey would pick up and not Cole. She still felt too ashamed to talk to her father.

"Hello? I mean, Red Hill Real Estate. Can I help you?"

"Stephanie?" Mary Kate said. "What are you doing there?"

"It feels like ten years of hard labor." Her sister's voice dropped to a whisper. "You shouldn't be calling me."

"I wasn't. I wanted to say sorry to Uncle Joey."

"I'll get him in a minute, but listen," Stephanie said excitedly. "Dad and your mum are at the hot springs right now."

"Get out!"

"It's true," Stephanie insisted. "I saw the note."

"After all the trouble we went to, they got together all by themselves," Mary Kate complained.

"I'm sure we helped. Do you think they'll kiss?"

"I hope so." Mary Kate sighed. "Wouldn't it be great if Dad proposed and they told us today they were getting married?"

"Would we be bridesmaids or flower girls?" Stephanie said.

"We're too old to be flower girls."

"But a bit young to be bridesmaids."

"We'd have to go shopping, whatever we were."

"Hang on," Stephanie said. "Someone just came in the door." She was back in a second. "Oh. My. God. It's Rafe Baldwyn!"

CHAPTER FOURTEEN

THE PHONE CLUNKED loudly as Stephanie
dropped it onto the desk instead of hanging
up. Mary Kate held the receiver away from
her. Then she put it back to her ear and
listened. She could hear everything—
Stephanie's excited babble and Rafe's
amused drawl.

"Mr. Baldwyn, would you mind… Could
I have your autograph?" There was the
sound of a page ripped off the memo,
followed by a pen dropping onto the floor
and the chair scraping and bumping into the
wall.

Mary Kate chuckled. *Calm down,
Stephanie.*

"Certainly," Rafe said. "Who are you?"

"Stephanie. I'm Mary Kate's half
sister."

"Ah, Mary Kate. Say hello to her for me, will you?"

"Hi, Rafe!" Mary Kate yelled through the phone but he didn't seem to hear her.

"Is Cole around?" the actor went on.

"He's not here right now," Stephanie said. "Oh, God. He's going to go mental when he finds out he's missed you. I'll call him on his mobile." She picked up the receiver.

Uh-oh, Mary Kate thought. She was going to be hung up on.

But Rafe intervened. "I just tried his mobile. It's not switched on."

"Oh. Okay." Clunk went the receiver onto the desk again. "Can I make you an appointment for say, five o'clock?"

"Get Joey!" Mary Kate screamed to no avail. It was so frustrating being in on the conversation and not being able to be heard.

"My flight to L.A. leaves in a few hours," Rafe said. "Tell Cole I'll catch up next time I'm in Australia."

"Wait!" Stephanie said. "Joey's here."

Rafe paused. "Joey?"

"My uncle. He can help you. He's an agent, too."

There was a long silence while Stephanie ran down the hall to Joey's office.

Then Mary Kate heard Joey's voice. She could imagine him sticking out his hand as he said, "G'day, Mr. Baldwyn. I'm Joey Roberts. I'd be happy to show you the Rasmussen estate. This is my— er, *your* lucky day."

JANE PUT THE TOP down on the Mazda and let the wind blow her hair around. The sun was shining through the trees. The radio blasted out Van Morrison's gloriously upbeat "Days Like This." And she couldn't wipe the lunatic grin off her face. Her limbs felt loose and languorous, her whole body meltingly soft and relaxed. She hadn't realized how stressed she'd become until Cole had given her the perfect antidote.

His Porsche snaked down the winding road ahead of her. She hoped he was enjoying the afterglow as much as she was. Their lovemaking hadn't been romantic so much as hot. Urgent. Time for them was limited. Soon she'd be moving to the city…

Which reminded her, had Jason received the check? Had he processed the paperwork? Her hand reached automatically into her purse for her mobile phone. Only to recall that she'd left it at home.

Jane tooted her horn as she turned off toward home while Cole continued on into town and his office. A few minutes later she stopped at the bottom of her driveway to pick up the mail. Tossing the sheaf of letters onto the passenger seat, she drove up to the house and parked.

She flipped down the sun visor to check her face in the mirror. Uh-oh. Swollen lips, whisker burn on her chin, the gleam in her eyes, the smile that wouldn't die… She was so busted.

"Mom!" Mary Kate came running out of the house. "Guess what?"

Jane slammed the visor up, grabbed the mail and climbed out of the car. "Hi, honey. How was your day? Did you get all those books packed?"

"Most of them. Guess what?" she repeated. "Joey sold a huge house to Rafe this afternoon for, like, millions of dollars."

"Not the Rasmussen estate." Jane stopped short. "This afternoon? How do you know?"

"I called to apologize to Joey but Stephanie answered. While I was talking to her, Rafe arrived. I could hear over the phone that Joey was going to show him the house." Mary Kate paused, looking sheepish. "I asked her to call me back afterward to let me know what happened. I know we weren't supposed to talk. I'm sorry…"

Jane wasn't listening. Numbly, she started moving again, up the steps onto the veranda, into the cool interior of the house. "Cole was counting on the commission from this sale. But now Joey will get the money."

"Cole was lucky Joey was there," Mary Kate said. "Rafe would have gone back to the States and no one would have made the sale."

"Joey did none of the legwork," Jane told her. "He made the sale simply by being in the right place at the right time." What would this mean? Would Cole still be able to purchase the farm?

Jane realized she was staring at the envelopes in her hand. The top letter bore the address of a Melbourne law office. Odd, it wasn't her aunt's legal firm. She started to rip it open.

Mary Kate hovered, her expression eager. "So how was it?"

Jane's hands stilled. "Pardon?"

"The spa pool. Did you and Cole have a good time together? Did he kiss you?"

"So Stephanie told you about that, too, did she?" Jane glanced away as heat rushed up her neck. "It's none of your business."

Her phone rang. Glad for the distraction, she said, "Excuse me," to Mary Kate and hurried to her office to take the call. She tossed the letters among the papers on her desk.

"Hello? Oh, hi, Walter." It was her boss at Moonray. "Thanks. The premiere did go smoothly, didn't it? Even Mia behaved herself." Then Walter told her about a new film being released in Australia next month and they spent a few minutes discussing publicity ideas. "I'll get on it right away. Ciao."

She hung up and looked around. "Mary Kate?" She must have given up and gone upstairs. Fine, Jane was just as happy not to answer any more questions about her afternoon with Cole, anyway. She reached for her phone again and punched in a number. "Otto. Hi, it's Jane."

And on to the next project.

COLE ROLLED HIS PEN between his fingers while Joey made the phone call to the owner of the Rasmussen estate. *He* should have been making that call. Bloody bad luck, that's what it was. He'd had the property on his books for over a year with nothing but wasted time to show for his efforts. Now the ink was barely dry on Joey's license and his little brother had made a sale of 8.5 million dollars.

Joey dropped the receiver back into the cradle. Still buzzing on the adrenaline, he extended a hand to Rafe. "The vendor has accepted your offer. Congratulations."

Why *wouldn't* the vendor accept? Rafe had paid the full asking price without blinking. What had possessed Cole to go to the hot springs without his mobile phone? He never went *anywhere* without his phone. Cole quietly stabbed a hole in the blotter on top of his desk.

Forcing a smile, he shook hands first with Rafe, then with Joey. "Congratulations."

He handed the documents to be signed over the desk to Joey, pointing out the remaining blanks to be filled in. In a particularly cruel twist he was forced to walk his brother through the contract procedures because Joey had so little experience.

Would he have done things differently had he known? Hot sex with Jane versus earning two hundred thousand dollars for an hour's work and the realization of his lifelong dream? Hmm…tough choice.

A smile crept onto his face as he replayed the afternoon in his mind. Jane seemed to enjoy herself, too. She *did* still make that erotic breathy moan in his ear. And strain toward him in anticipation of him entering her.

The pen in his hand snapped.

Wake up, idiot! He wasn't going to get

the girl. He wasn't going to get the farm. He was going to be stuck in this bloody office for the rest of his sorry life.

"Cole?" Joey glanced up from the document, his gaze anxiously searching Cole's face. "Are you all right?"

"Sure." Cole tossed the fragments of plastic into the bin and reached for a tissue to wipe his hands. He met Joey's gaze and realized how much his cocky young brother still looked to him for direction. That Joey was looking to him *right now,* for assurance that he'd done the right thing in making the sale in Cole's absence. What could he say but, "Good job, mate."

"I have a plane to catch," Rafe said, checking his watch. "I'll be back in a month to go fishing in my new dam." Rising, he shook hands with Cole. Joey walked him out.

Wearily Cole rubbed his hands over his face, wondering what the hell he was going to do now. From the doorway, Joey cleared his throat. Cole glanced up.

"About the commission," Joey began. "We'll split it, fifty-fifty."

Cole shook his head. "You know the protocol. He who makes the sale gets the reward. That's the real estate business."

"But we're brothers," Joey argued. "The standard procedure doesn't apply."

"If I expect *you* to follow the rules then *I* have to follow them, too." Cole mustered a tight smile. "Now get out of here before I change my mind."

WHEN JANE HAD FINISHED making her work calls, she rang Jason. He'd received her check, deposited it in his agency's trust account and was processing the paperwork.

Mary Kate was lying on her bed reading when Jane went upstairs. Empty boxes sat on the floor, untouched, while her dresser was cluttered with brushes, jewelry and assorted junk.

"We're moving out tomorrow," Jane reminded her from the doorway. "Why aren't you packing? When you're done, I need you to help me clean up downstairs so the place is presentable for Cole and Stephanie."

"I thought Cole doesn't have enough money now that Joey got the Rasmussen commission," Mary Kate said. "I thought we wouldn't be going."

"He's paid the deposit. He'll find the rest, somehow." She hoped for his sake that was true. "It's happening," she added gently. "We're moving out, they're moving in."

"But what about Stephanie's birthday party?" Mary Kate asked, looking troubled. "We can't leave before that."

Jane sat on the bed and brushed back Mary Kate's hair. "We'll come back for it, don't worry."

"So you and Cole aren't getting married?"

Jane took the magazine from her daughter. "Sweetheart, where do you get these romantic notions? Now, please start getting your things packed."

After dinner Jane cleaned the kitchen until it sparkled. A new stove, sink and fridge and a fresh coat of creamy paint gave the room a bright contemporary feel. Cole's scarred mountain-ash table and a few family photos on the wall would provide that homey feeling all kitchens should have.

Well, maybe not *all* kitchens. But the tiny galley kitchen in her new apartment would be more than adequate for the simple meals she and Mary Kate would require.

When Jane finally finished cleaning and packing, the house was silent. Glancing at her watch, she saw it was after eleven. Sighing, she rose and went upstairs to check on Mary Kate. No light shone beneath her door and when Jane peeked in she heard the soft sound of her daughter's sleeping breath. The moonlight filtering through a crack in the curtains illuminated the bare dresser and packed boxes. Jane breathed a sigh of relief.

Moving quietly over the creaky hardwood floor, she went to her room to pack the last items into her suitcases. She tried to tell herself she was glad to finally be putting this house behind her. Although in a sense, she wasn't. Cole and Stephanie would live here. Mary Kate would visit. Jane and Cole would…

What? This afternoon they'd worked through some important issues. Her heart felt lighter than it had in years. Misguided or not, Cole *had* loved her thirteen years ago. True, he hadn't said anything about his current feelings for her. It was possible that this afternoon had simply been about satisfying curiosity and a lingering case of teenage lust.

Her packing finished, she went back to the kitchen and took the garbage out to the big bin next to the garage. A possum crashed through the branches of a nearby gum tree, all gleaming round eyes and bushy tail. Drawn by the glow of a bright pewter half-moon rising above the cypress trees, Jane walked around to the front of the house. The hills and valley looked soft and peaceful bathed in silver.

Regardless of what happened with Cole, she would miss this house and the land. *Couldn't we all live together somewhere?* Mary Kate's words came back to her. *Yes,* her heart answered. Here, at Cockatoo Ridge, where they all belonged. Did she and Cole belong together? Doubt crept in as she thought of all the times he'd call L.A. to talk to Mary Kate, never speaking to her more than was necessary. Was that because he hadn't wanted to foster a relationship that couldn't be? Or because he no longer cared? It had been three years since his divorce. If he'd wanted to, he could have tried to resurrect their relationship. But all he'd ever been interested in was Mary Kate.

The familiar purr of Cole's Porsche sounded faintly and a moment later headlights came over the rise in the driveway. He parked and turned the motor off. Quiet fell; all she could hear was the ticking of the cooling engine. And another sound that took her a moment to identify. The rapid beating of her heart.

The car door opened and Cole's lanky frame emerged wearing a lightweight shirt that moved in the slight breeze and dark jeans. His shoes crunched on the gravel as he came toward her. Without a word he took her in his arms.

Jane's doubts were pushed to the back of her mind by the warmth of his embrace. This afternoon Cole's kisses had been hot and urgent; now he was deliberate and tender. Her heart tumbled over as waves of love flowed through her.

Finally he drew back to look into her eyes. "Hi."

"Hi, yourself." Shyness overtook her for once in her life. "What are you doing here? Where's Stephanie?"

"At her mum's. I couldn't sleep for thinking about you." His fingers moved gently over her lips, her cheeks, tracing the lines of her nose as if discovering her all over again. "Are you still leaving in the morning?"

Jane pressed her face to his chest, feeling the strong steady thump of his heart. "Yes."

"I wish you wouldn't go," he said roughly.

"Oh, Cole." She swept her arms around his neck and lifted her face to be kissed. He held her so close she could feel every inch of his long strong body against hers. "Let's go inside."

They made love in her aunt's high brass bed with the moonlight streaming through the window. Muffled sighs and soft creaks were the only sounds to mar the quiet of the old house. Jane barely spoke, so conscious was she that her daughter was in the bedroom just down the hall.

In silence, Cole gathered her close, kissing her neck then moving lower to her breasts, suckling her nipples until she was weak with desire. Then he kissed her some more, rousing her to energetic athletic sex. She peaked, biting her lip to keep from crying out, then slid, limp and damp, to wallow in a puddle of bliss.

"No more," she panted, flat on her back, arms and legs spread-eagled. "I can't take any more."

But after they'd slept for a few hours, with her spooned against his back, *she* was the one to slide her hand over his hip. Cole moaned, semiconscious as she stroked him until sensation moved through his groin, stirring him. *If this was a dream, let him sleep forever.*

Before long, he realized it wasn't a dream and then he wasn't content to lie there passively. Rolling over, he captured her beneath him. "You can't have any more. You can't take it."

Giggling, she nodded. "Yes, I can."

As it turned out, she could. And did.

The night proceeded in fragments. Waking, making love till they were exhausted, sleeping some more. The moon set, stars came out. Finally dawn made the room glow pink, bringing the ripe wheat color back to Jane's hair, the rose to her cheeks and lips. Cole lay on his side and watched her sleeping face.

Her eyes fluttered open and she yawned. "Morning."

Cole tried to memorize her features in case what he had to say would ruin their budding romance.

"Jane, I have to tell you something."

Her smiled faded. "What is it?"

"I can't buy the farm. I banked on getting that commission and now…" He sucked in a breath. "If I go into debt that deeply and can't service the mortgage I could end up losing the agency."

"It's not fair that Joey got the commission on the Rasmussen estate," she began angrily, propping herself up on one arm. "He should share it with you."

"He was on the spot and made the sale.

That's all that counts in the end," Cole said, trying not to feel bitter. "It's standard practice among real estate agents."

"But you did all the groundwork," Jane persisted. "Joey never would have made that sale if you hadn't talked to Rafe about the property and convinced him it was worth coming out to view."

"I know it doesn't seem right but there's nothing I can do," Cole said. "At least Joey won't be borrowing off me for a while." Talking things over helped ease his resentment, even if it wouldn't bring that commission back.

Jane was silent for a moment. "So there's no way you can afford the farm, not even if you sell the house you're living in?"

Cole shook his head. "I've been over the figures a hundred times. It's just too much for me."

"Then I'll lower my price. How much can you pay?"

"I can't let you do that. I won't accept charity. The farm will sell sooner or later for the asking price, I'm confident of that. I'll forfeit my deposit, of course."

"No!"

"You need that money for your deposit on the apartment. Legally, you have every right to it." He curled a lock of her hair around his finger. With a sad smile he let it slip away and spring back to her neck.

"There's a three-day cooling-off period," she said. "You can still back out."

"Real estate agents don't get a cooling-off period when they purchase property. We're supposed to know what we're doing." He glanced at the clock and pushed back the covers. "I'd better go."

Cole dressed and went quietly downstairs. He kissed Jane goodbye at the door. Although his heart was heavy with disappointment over losing the farm, he could be glad of one thing—Jane was back in his life. "I'll call you later."

Instead, she rang him, shortly after nine o'clock. He'd barely settled behind his desk with a cup of extra-strong coffee when Millie put the call through. His pleasure at hearing from her made his voice rough. "Missed me already?"

Her short angry laugh took him by

surprise. "What kind of games are you playing with me now, Cole?" she demanded, her voice nothing like the loving tones he'd heard from her last night. "Do you get some kind of kick out of making me love you then delivering a death blow?"

Bewildered, he set his cup down on a pencil, and coffee slopped over the side. "What are you talking about?"

"I received a letter yesterday from Morrison, Morrison and Glebe. I didn't get around to opening it until this morning."

Oh God. Ice flowed through his veins. "Jane—"

"The letter was from your lawyer warning me you're starting legal proceedings to gain *sole custody* of Mary Kate." Her voice snapped with anger. "Well, let me tell you, Cole Roberts, you're going to have the fight of your life."

CHAPTER FIFTEEN

COLE SWORE under his breath, mentally kicking himself for not getting back to Ron to put the brakes on. "I can explain. I did contact my lawyer a few weeks ago when it seemed as if you wouldn't let me see Mary Kate. I've changed my mind since then. With everything that's been happening in the past couple of weeks, it completely slipped my mind. I'll call straightaway and cancel the request."

"*Sole* custody?" Jane repeated, incensed. "How could you do that to me? I was willing to give you access."

"I never wanted to take Mary Kate away from you," Cole said. "My lawyer convinced me that starting out with an ambit claim of sole custody would strengthen my chances of getting joint custody. I thought it was a mistake at the time."

"Damn right it was a mistake. And guess what else happened? A *horse* arrived this morning." Jane's voice rose to a near-hysterical pitch. "You're resorting to bribery in case the judge asks Mary Kate which parent she'd prefer to live with."

"I'm telling you, this will never make it to family court or mediation or whatever they do nowadays," Cole said, struggling to remain calm while his anger flared at her accusations. "I wasn't trying to bribe Mary Kate into staying in Red Hill with me. I simply wanted to give my daughter, whom I've hardly seen in years, a gift."

"The timing couldn't be worse if you'd tried. Or maybe you knew exactly what you were doing," Jane went on angrily. "The moving van is here and the men are loading up my stuff. Mary Kate's out in the barn with that animal, refusing to leave for Melbourne. I want you to get over here and take the horse away."

Cole rubbed between his eyes where a headache was rapidly forming. "Can we deal with one thing at a time? Forget about the custody application. It was a mistake."

"Forget? How can I forget? You could have at least talked to me before you went to a lawyer."

"I tried," he said, recalling the day they'd tasted wine in his shed. "You wouldn't listen."

"Do you have any idea what it felt like to get that letter? It stopped my heart cold." Mingled anguish and anger turned her voice ragged. "After we'd made love…and held each other and…and said things. It was the biggest slap in the face…"

"I'll fix this," he insisted. "I'll call my lawyer and tell him I'm not going ahead with the custody application. Jane, we've got so much going for us—"

"Not anymore," she said, tears clogging her throat and making her words indistinct. "The damage is done. How can I trust you?"

"Jane—"

She hung up.

Cole dropped his head in his hands, his fingers spearing through his hair. This couldn't be happening.

Pulling himself together, he called Ron and canceled the custody suit. Then he grabbed his car keys and told Millie to cancel all his appointments.

JANE WAS BRINGING suitcases out to the veranda for the moving men to load onto the truck, when she heard the Porsche pull into the driveway. Good, he'd come for the horse. He got out of his car and started toward her. She steeled herself. Before he could speak to her, Mary Kate came running out of the barn and threw herself into his arms, thanking him for the horse. Cole pulled her into a hug, lifting her feet off the ground.

Pain knifed through Jane. His top priority all along had been Mary Kate. Then Cole turned and started for the house and she clenched her fists. She wished this day was over and she was out of this crummy town.

"Mary Kate, can you go back to the barn?" Jane said when the girl started to follow him. "Your father and I need to talk. Alone."

"Excuse me, ma'am," a burly red-haired man in gray overalls interrupted. "Is all the furniture going?"

"Yes," Jane told him. "Everything marked with masking tape is going to the storage facility. The rest will come with me to the apartment."

The moving men clumped up the steps and across the wooden veranda, into the house.

Mary Kate ignored Jane's request to leave her and Cole alone, asking eagerly, "Are you going to talk about moving in together?"

"Hardly," Jane said. "Cole and I won't be seeing each other again."

"What?" Mary Kate cried. "After everything Stephanie and I did to make you and Cole fall in love?"

"You can't make someone fall in love, no matter how much you want it to happen," Jane said. "I learned that a long time ago."

Cole took a step toward Jane. "I *did* love you."

"Did you?" she said coldly. "I wonder now."

The moving men came out of the house carrying the couch, forcing them to step aside.

"Let's go over there. Mary Kate, go to the barn." Jane led the way across the yard to the apple trees on the edge of the slope. Cole followed. Mary Kate moved off toward the barn then stopped about ten meters away, watching them. Jane turned to Cole. "I have a proposition for you."

"What is it?" He crossed his arms over his chest, his jaw set tight.

"Swear, in writing, that you relinquish all claim to custody of Mary Kate. And you can have the farm for the price my aunt paid for it fourteen years ago plus ten percent."

"I already stopped the custody application," he began angrily.

"How do I know you won't set it in motion again the next time you're ticked with me?" she demanded. "Or if you decide I'm not raising Mary Kate right? That letter from your lawyer came out of the blue. I won't risk being blindsided again."

Cole glanced over to Mary Kate. Jane

followed his gaze and saw her daughter had shuffled closer. She was about to tell her to move off, when Cole spoke again.

"Even if I signed such an agreement, I doubt it would be legally binding," he said.

"I guess I'm relying on you to have *some* ethics," Jane said. "Take the farm, leave my daughter to me. It's not like you won't ever see her. But even if you went to court, odds are I'd retain custody."

"Maybe you *should* take it, Dad. You love this farm." Mary Kate spoke up, only a few feet away now. She'd obviously heard enough to know what was going on.

Love and anguish raced over Cole's face as he shook his head. "I don't want the farm that badly. I want you, Mary Kate." He turned to Jane. "And I want you, if you'd only believe me."

"How *can* I believe you?" Jane asked, wrapping her arms around herself.

Crying, Mary Kate ran to Cole and took shelter under his arm. "Why are you doing this, Mom? You're supposed to love each other."

Jane wavered. Then she looked at Cole,

who'd broken her heart not once but twice. "What are you going to do?" she demanded. "Take it or leave it?"

"Leave it." He looked like death.

"If that's the way you want it," Jane said stiffly. "Come, Mary Kate. We're leaving."

"No!" Mary Kate shouted. "I'm not going. I'm staying with Dad." She clutched Cole's waist as if she was chaining herself to him.

Cole smoothed her hair back from her tearstained face and kissed her forehead. "Go with your mother, sweetheart. I'll see you soon. I promise."

In the end, Jane had no choice but to drag Mary Kate, crying and screaming, away from her father.

JANE LET HERSELF INTO her brand-new Docklands apartment. Boxes sat against the wall in every room. She simply hadn't had the time or, she had to admit, the inclination, to unpack. Every time she opened the vertical blinds and looked out over the concrete expanse to the harbor, she had to remind herself what a fabulous new home she had.

Her mobile phone rang. She tucked it under her ear as she sorted through the mail. "Jane, here."

A husky female voice said, "Hello, darling. I'm back."

"Mia," Jane greeted her listlessly. "How was Bora-Bora?"

"Dreadful." Mia made a shuddering sound. "The villa was on stilts at the end of a boardwalk a million miles from the shore. There was water *everywhere.* I'm agoraphobic. Did you know that, darling?"

"No, I didn't," Jane murmured. Bills, bills, bills. She tossed them unopened onto the hall table and wandered into the kitchen.

"Neither did I until I got there. They had to call the air ambulance to rush me to the Marriott Hotel in Papeete," Mia said. "But listen, I know how you can help me."

"Anything for you, Mia," Jane said through gritted teeth. "You know that." She found a tub of yogurt in the fridge and peeled off the foil top.

"I need that man's phone number. You know who I mean, big shoulders, yummy green eyes, gorgeously tousled hair."

"*Cole?* What do you want with him?" Jane tried to keep the outrage out of her voice. *She* had tousled his hair. His hair belonged to *her.* Even if she never wanted to see him again as long as she lived. Jane stabbed a spoon into the creamy dairy product.

Mia's laugh tinkled irritatingly. "If you must know, he invited me to his daughter's birthday lunch, and I forgot what day it was."

"This Sunday." So he'd invited Mia. He must have done that the night of the premiere. Not surprisingly, he hadn't mentioned the party to Jane since she'd left Red Hill. Not that she had any intention of going even though she knew he'd planned a large gathering with adults as well as children. Jane had already told Mary Kate she could go. The girl had been sullen and uncommunicative ever since that last horrible day at the farm.

"Do you have Cole's phone number?" Mia was asking. "I might go down there tomorrow and let him give me some of his wine."

"I'll e-mail it to your phone." Grimly,

she copied and sent Cole's number. "There, you should have it."

"*Thank* you." Mia added, "I'm not stepping on any toes, am I, darling?"

"Not mine," Jane replied lightly. "Cole is my daughter's father but he's nothing to me."

COLE UNLOCKED the door to the farmhouse and let himself into the silent hallway. He was having Stephanie's birthday party here—Jane had agreed to it by e-mail—but he wanted to say goodbye alone. He walked through the empty rooms, his foot-steps echoing beneath the high ceiling. He could picture his leather couch in front of the fireplace, the wing chair to one side and a reading lamp behind it.

He'd imagined moving back to the farmhouse for so many years. For a split second, he'd almost been tempted to accept Jane's offer. But not really. Not when the personal cost was so high.

He ran a hand over the top of the polished marble mantelpiece, his fingertip finding the tiny nick he'd accidentally put there with a poker when he was ten years old. So many memories had been made, so many changes had taken place in this house, some good, some bad, but all part of the continuity that flowed from his great-grandfather through the generations. And ended with him.

Jane had done a lot in the four weeks she'd been there. The entire downstairs wore a coat of fresh paint. The bathroom had been redone and the wiring was up to code. The kitchen gleamed with brand-new appliances. Even the garden beds around the front of the house had been weeded.

Jane had said Mary Kate could come to Stephanie's birthday party and would be allowed to spend the weekend. Ron had advised him to go ahead with custody proceedings but he'd declined, not wanting Mary Kate to be a pawn in his dispute with Jane.

Cole's cell phone rang. He half hoped it wasn't someone wanting to look at a house. He was sick to death of real estate. Not that he could afford to turn down a po-tential client. "Hello?"

"Cole, darling, this is Mia. I'm back in Melbourne."

"That's, uh…great," Cole replied, surprised, flattered and dismayed all at the same time.

"When can I see you?" she asked huskily and he could imagine her lush red lips thrust into a sexy pout.

Not for one moment did Cole believe Mia MacDonald was interested in him. She must have an ulterior motive. What could it be? "I really don't know. I'm very busy with work. I'll give you a call."

"But I'm bringing you business. I want one, too, darling."

"One, what?"

"A home in the country," Mia explained. "A retreat from Hollywood. Like Rafe's."

Oh, so that was it. "In that case I'll look over our listings and see if there's anything suitable."

"Tomorrow you can take me to lunch then we'll look at houses together," she informed him. "And, darling, try not to sound so much like a real estate agent."

Before Cole could protest, she hung up. Shaking his head, he clicked off his phone. MARY KATE BOOTED UP her computer and logged on to an Internet chat room to talk to Stephanie. Typing with two fingers, she wrote:

My new school sucks. This apartment sucks. Mom is *so* not happy but she won't admit it.

Stephanie's reply appeared letter by letter:

It's awful here without you. Dad is going out with Mia MacDonald for lunch today.

Mary Kate stared at the screen. Mia MacDonald. Jeez, how could her mom compete with a movie star?

You've got to sabotage their date.

No way. I'll be grounded for the rest of my life.

Fake your own death. Slash Dad's tires.

Face it. We're stuffed.

I'm going to tell Mom.

What can she do? Even if she wanted to do anything.

I don't know. She's our only chance.

Mary Kate signed off and went in search of her mother. Jane was curled up on the love seat in the lounge room, watching a kids' educational game show. A half-empty cup of tea was cooling at her elbow.

"Mom?" Mary Kate sat on the matching chair.

Jane continued to stare at the screen. "Yes?"

"Cole is having lunch with Mia MacDonald."

"I'm not surprised. I gave her his number," Jane replied in a flat voice. The game-show host asked one panel of kids a question and Jane answered, "Kangaroos."

Mary Kate moved to block the TV. "Mom! You're not eating, you're not sleeping. You're not communicating. You've got to snap out of it. What are you going to do about Dad and Mia?"

"Cole is free to go out with anyone he wants as far as I'm concerned. In fact, he and Mia deserve each other." She peered around Mary Kate, listening to the next question. "The 2000 Sydney Olympics."

Mary Kate grabbed the TV control and turned the show off. "You and Dad are in love with each other. Why don't you get that?"

Jane sipped her tea. "He's not in love with me. He only wants you. And FYI, I'm not in love with him."

Mary Kate threw up her hands. "You're wrong. You're so in love with Cole you're having a nervous breakdown. You're just too stubborn to see it."

Mary Kate stomped off back to her room. Jane reached for the remote, turning the TV back on. But she couldn't see the screen because her eyes were blurred with tears.

COLE HAD ALMOST finished the Sudoku when the outer-door buzzer sounded. He heard Millie shriek then gush with excitement, her babble all but drowning out the husky feminine voice of the visitor. Cole took a deep breath, mentally preparing himself for the ordeal ahead.

Rising, he walked out to greet the actress. She exuded sex appeal in a low-cut clinging blouse, miniskirt and five-inch heels. Millie clutched a piece of paper he assumed bore the actress's autograph.

"Mia," Cole said. "Nice to see you again."

"Darling!" Arms outstretched, Mia waited for him to come to her, holding her cheek to be kissed. "What a charming little backwater town you have down here."

"We like it." Cole leaned over Millie's desk and said in a low voice, "Close your mouth." Then, straightening, he turned back to Mia. "I've booked a table at a winery for lunch—"

The door opened. Jane entered with Mary Kate close behind. Instantly Cole forgot all about Mia as his daughter rushed into his arms. "Hey, easy," he said, holding her. "I'm glad to see you, too." He glanced up at Jane. "Shouldn't she be in school?"

"Apparently all they were doing this afternoon was watching a movie for English, which she's already seen. I suppose it wasn't right to take her out, but—"

"I don't mind," Cole said. "Can she stay for lunch?"

"Darling," Mia broke in. "You're taking *me* to lunch."

"She can stay for lunch," Jane said, flinging a deadly glance at Mia. "And dinner. And overnight if it's convenient."

"It's always convenient." Cole turned to Mia. "Look, I'm really sorry but I haven't seen my daughter in a couple of weeks. You understand, don't you?"

"What about the properties you were going to show me?" Mia pouted.

"Joey can show you," Mary Kate piped up.

Cole groaned inwardly. Another big commission out the window. "That's right," he agreed. "Joey can show you."

Joey happily took Mia off Cole's hands, even offering to take her to lunch. Mary

Kate went off to Cole's office to call Stephanie, leaving Cole alone with Jane.

"Thank you for bringing her down here," he said stiffly. "I wasn't expecting her until Sunday."

Her mission accomplished, Jane stepped to the door, as if she couldn't wait to get away from him. "It's Friday tomorrow and she has a curriculum day, so she has a long weekend. She's packed enough clothes to stay through the weekend. If that's convenient."

"It's fine. In fact, it's perfect. Joey was planning on fulfilling his end of the bargain he made at my house the night everyone was over for the barbecue. He wants to take the girls to Luna Park on Saturday for Stephanie's birthday."

Pausing in the doorway, Jane twisted her hands. "I don't want Mary Kate to get caught in the middle of our quarrel. I…handled things badly that last day at the farm. She should never have witnessed our argument. I just want her to be happy."

"That makes two of us." Cole paused. "You could stay for the weekend, too. There's plenty of room."

"I have to attend the Grand Prix tomorrow," Jane said, edging outside. "Moonray Productions is releasing a racing film and we're using the event for publicity."

She backed out the door. And then she was gone.

CHAPTER SIXTEEN

JOEY RETURNED to the office in a little over two hours. He came into Cole's office and shut the door, peering through the glass wall to make sure Mia stayed where he'd left her in reception. He turned to Cole, looking harried. "You have to take her back."

Cole set aside the contract note he was preparing. After lunch he'd dropped Mary Kate off at his house to wait for Stephanie to come home from school. "What's the problem?"

"She thinks I'm her personal slave," Joey complained. "She had me on my knees, polishing the toes of her shoes when they got a speck of mud on them at that new house lot out on Brandywine Way."

Cole grinned and leaned back in his chair. "She's a real sweetheart, isn't she?"

"And she keeps pushing her boobs into my face. She almost suffocated me when I buckled her seat belt for her."

"Which you did because…?"

"She was afraid of breaking a nail." Joey held out his hands pressed together as if in prayer. "Please, Cole. I've been good lately, haven't I? You aren't still punishing me for my past sins?"

Cole took pity on him and reached for his jacket. "Which properties have you shown her?"

Joey told him. "They're all the ones I could think of in her bracket."

"Leave her with me," Cole said. "I know of one other property she might be interested in."

UNDER A STRIPED MARQUEE, Jane balanced a champagne glass in one hand and an oyster on the half shell in the other, while she listened to a woman in a big hat trill on. She sneaked a glance at her watch and wondered when she could decently make her escape. In the background, Formula One engines whined as the drivers did warm-up laps around the temporary track encircling Albert Lake.

Out of the corner of her eye, Jane glimpsed a familiar brown head scanning the crowd of chattering women. Oh, God, what was *he* doing here? Cole lifted a glass of champagne from a passing waiter and started toward her.

She turned to listen more attentively to what the woman was saying. She was aware that Cole was coming closer every second, and was extremely annoyed to find her heart speeding up. She'd done her best to put him out of her mind these past two weeks. Seeing him yesterday had been difficult and to encounter him two days in a row seemed downright cruel.

"Excuse me, ma'am." Cole smiled apologetically at the older woman. "I need to borrow Ms. Linden. Film business, you know." He took Jane's arm and pulled her away, murmuring, "So this is where female rev-heads hang out."

Jane tugged out of his grip. "How did *you* get in?"

He put his hand next to his mouth.

"Don't tell anyone, but I'm actually Rafe Baldwyn disguised as a real estate agent from the country."

Jane gave him the once-over. He was wearing a suit and white shirt with no tie. His jaw was cleanly shaved but his hair still wore that sexy bedroom look. He did look more like an actor than a country Realtor. "So Rafe gave you his ticket. You must have been persuasive."

Cole ignored that to eye her oyster. "Still on the aphrodisiacs, I see."

Glaring at him, Jane debated throwing the oyster away then decided that would be a waste. She tipped it into her mouth then took a drink of champagne. "Did you bring Mia?"

"No, I wanted to talk to you." Cole wiped away a drop of wine from her bottom lip with his thumb.

Flustered, she dabbed pointlessly at the spot with her napkin. "What about?"

"I have a proposition for you," Cole said. "Can we go somewhere we don't have to shout?"

She should tell him to take his proposition and shove it. But she was curious.

"You'll have to make it quick. I'm supposed to be talking up the new film."

She led him out of the park to a bistro on Clarendon Street. Cole ordered another glass of wine and Jane asked for a latte. When the waiter left, she put on her briskest tone. "What was it you wanted to talk about?"

Cole reached across the table for her hand. "I've missed you."

Jane pulled away, trying to ignore the tingle sparked by his touch. "That's not what you drove all the way to Melbourne to say."

"No, it's not."

Damn. Jane lifted her chin. "What then?"

"First, I've found a buyer for the farm. Someone who will pay full price."

Jane waited while the waiter set down her coffee and Cole's glass of Shiraz. "Who?"

"Mia."

"Mia, among the cows and sheep? I don't believe it. You know what she's after, don't you?"

"A country retreat?"

"No, *you,* of course." Jane shook her head,

amazed he could be so obtuse. "And it's all your fault. You let her drool over you at the premiere. You *kissed* her. I suppose you're even going to waive your commission."

"Wrong again. I'm not waiving my commission. And I didn't kiss Mia, she kissed me. Even so, she isn't interested in me except as an occasional escort. And let me tell you, I'm not cut out for that role. What she wants is to be neighbors with Rafe." He pulled a fat envelope from his inside pocket and laid it on the table. "Here's the contract note, already signed by Mia, plus a check. I doubt hers will bounce."

Jane turned the envelope over, confused at her emotions. She realized she'd hoped that somehow Cole would find the money to buy the farm. Or accept her offer. "The house is so old. I can't believe she'd want to live there."

He grimaced. "She's planning to tear it down and rebuild."

"You're willing to go along with that?" Jane was shocked.

Cole shrugged. "You asked me to sell your property. That's what I'm doing."

"What's this about a proposition?"

"Not a proposition so much as a proposal." He pushed his wineglass out of the way and leaned across the table, taking her hands. This time she didn't pull away. "Marry me. If you want to live in Melbourne that's where we'll live. This is not about me wanting custody of Mary Kate. I *love* you. I want us to be a family. Nothing else matters. Not the farm, not the vineyard."

"I...I don't know what to say," Jane said, taken aback. "How can I believe you?"

"All I have to give up is my life in Red Hill, but I'm willing to do that if it'll prove how much I want to be with you."

Jane hesitated. Part of her wanted desperately to say yes but something inside held her back. Something that told her what he was saying was just plain wrong. "No."

"What?" His fingers lost their grasp on her hand as she stood up. "Will you think about it?"

"I..." She couldn't think at all. "I've got to go."

"Jane…" He pushed a hand through his hair. Then he handed her the envelope. "Don't forget the contract note. Sign it and return it to me."

FROM THE HEAD of the table Cole gazed down two rows of smiling faces preparing to feast on the groaning platters of barbe-cued meats and salads. Family and friends so numerous they'd had to put three tables in a row at the edge of the farmyard with the view over the hills. Valerie was here, with Joey and Crystal on one side and Leslie and Fergus and their two little boys opposite. Audrey and Bert sat on the far end. William Lasky was chatting with Rafe Baldwyn about the local footy team. William's wife, Lorraine, a herbalist, was exchanging natural-beauty tips with Mia. William and Lorraine's three children were clustered at the far end. Millie was there with her new boyfriend, an appren-tice cheese maker. Other guests included a local vintner and his wife, some teacher friends of Leslie's and half a dozen school friends of Stephanie's.

Valerie leaned forward to speak to Cole. "I don't see Jane. I thought since you're having Stephanie's birthday lunch here she might be coming."

"She gave permission by e-mail for us to use Cockatoo Ridge," Cole explained. "There's plenty of space for the kids to run around, plus a great view."

"You did invite her, didn't you?" Valerie persisted.

"Yes, Mother." He'd invited her to share his *life*. "She had something else to do, I guess." He'd set a place for her but didn't really expect her to show up.

Joey filled his glass with red wine from one of the many bottles that dotted the table. He leaned over to Cole.

"I showed the Burnside place to Audrey and Bert. I think they're going to buy it."

"Don't hold your breath," Cole said. "They're very picky."

"This time is different." Joey glanced down the table to where the O'Keefes were sitting. "They're that close to saying yes. I can scent a sale in the air. God, it's so exciting."

"Better than closing the deal on a mul-timillion-dollar estate?" Cole asked wryly.

"*Way* better. Selling the estate to Rafe was like shooting a duck in a pond because you'd set the deal up. Snagging Audrey and Bert is like capturing a couple of rare butterflies." Joey paused to eat an olive. "I've got a proposition for you, mate."

Everyone had a proposition these days. "What is it?"

"You know how you wanted to buy this place?" Joey said, spreading his hand to encompass the farmhouse and the land. "What if I bought into Red Hill Real Estate using my commission from the Rasmussen sale? I'd be a real partner. And you would have the capital to buy Cockatoo Ridge."

A thrill of excitement ran through Cole. "How do I know you wouldn't blow the trust account at the casino?"

"I haven't gambled in weeks. I'm getting counseling and I really think I can beat this." Joey put an arm around Crystal. "I've got another reason to walk the straight and narrow. We're going to have a baby."

Valerie shrieked. "You never told me!"

"I'm telling you now," Joey said.

"We're getting married at Easter," Crystal added.

"Congratulations." Cole raised a glass. "You're growing up at last."

"This doesn't mean I have to start wearing a tie, does it?" Joey said, alarmed, sparking laughter from his family.

"When are we going to eat?" Valerie asked when she'd stopped chuckling. "Everyone's getting sloshed."

"We're waiting for Stephanie and Mary Kate," Cole replied. "She and Mary Kate rode over along the creek. There they are now," he added, seeing them come out of the barn.

Two red-cheeked breathless girls raced to the empty chairs reserved for them in the middle of the table.

Cole rose and tapped his knife on his glass to quell the buzz of conversation and laughter. When everyone had quieted down, he spoke. "Thank you all for coming today to help celebrate Stephanie's twelfth birthday. It's a particularly special birthday. As most of you know she's recently become acquainted with her half sister, Mary Kate, who is with us today. So without further ado, I'll invite you all to enjoy your meal."

He'd resumed his seat, when a familiar growling motor sounded behind the cypress trees. A minute later a black Mazda climbed the hill. Cole waited, not quite daring to believe Jane had come.

"Mom!" Mary Kate left her place and ran over to where her mother parked behind Joey's Toyota.

Jane got out of the car, her long blond hair waving around the shoulders of her latte-colored jersey dress. She opened the trunk of her car and hauled out a brand-new saddle tied with a big red bow.

Of course. She'd come for Stephanie's birthday.

She had something else sticking out of her purse. The large yellow envelope containing the contract note. His heart sank. She'd signed it and brought it back to him. Joey's suggestion had come too late.

Jane brought the saddle around to

Stephanie and wished her happy birthday. His daughter exclaimed over the gleaming leather then put her arms around Jane to thank her with a big hug. Over her head, Jane's gaze flicked to his and her lips curved briefly. Then she glanced away as if she was unsure what she was doing here.

The only empty seat was at the opposite end of the three tables. Mary Kate took her hand and pulled her over there and made her sit. Immediately Jane was caught up in conversation with Audrey. For the next hour everyone was eating and drinking, talking and laughing. Cole's eyes went frequently to Jane. Sometimes she met his gaze, then glanced away. Sometimes he simply looked at her while pretending to listen to Valerie or Joey. It seemed impossible that she shouldn't be his, that after all these years, their reunion was going to fade away to nothing.

Gradually the platters emptied; appetites were sated. Leslie picked up some empty plates and carried them into the house. Cole moved along the table to her spot, two chairs closer to Jane. There he got caught up in a discussion with Richard, the winemaker, over cool climate grapes. When he glanced up again, Jane was three chairs nearer the center, on the other side, chatting with Rafe.

The children left the table and dispersed, to the stable, to the creek, to play cricket on the lawn. In ones and twos the adults re-arranged themselves to chat, to take a walk, to have another glass of wine.

Jane laughed at Rafe extolling the virtues of country living as if he'd invented it.

"You should rethink that city apartment. The air is so much fresher out here." He paused to light a cigarette. "Cole hasn't taken his eyes off you all afternoon. Have you even spoken to him?"

Jane fingered a dessert spoon, shot a glance at Cole. He was still one and a half table lengths away. His face glowed in the slanting rays of the sun. His smile was warm, his laughter rich. He looked like all the dreams in her life that hadn't come her way. Which wasn't to say she'd had a bad life. Just different from the one she'd once hoped for. But it wasn't over yet. "I'm working up to it."

"What's wrong?" Rafe put his hand over hers. "Don't you love him?"

Before she could say anything, Mia sank gracefully into the chair on Rafe's other side. "Darling," she said to Jane. "Are you going to sell me this property or not? Cole says he has another place he can show me."

Jane followed Mia's gaze. Cole was clapping Richard on the shoulder and rising out of his chair.

Rafe winked at Jane and tugged Mia to her feet. "Come down to the creek with me."

"Ooh, darling!" Mia linked her arm with his and let him lead her over the crest of the hill.

"Just keep your eye out for snakes," Rafe added carelessly.

"Snakes?" Mia repeated. "They're not poisonous, are they?"

"If you get to the hospital straightaway there's a chance you'll survive." Rafe's fading voice was punctuated with Mia's shrieks of alarm.

Jane glanced up to see Cole moving

toward the empty seat next to her. Then William waylaid him and Leslie dropped into the chair Rafe had vacated.

"I'm so glad you came today," Leslie said, giving Jane a hug. "Thank you for the beautiful saddle you gave Stephanie. It's very generous of you."

"I'm sure she'll get good use out of it." Jane reached into her red leather tote and removed a box. "This is for you. My aunt would have wanted you to have it."

Leslie's face lit as she removed a slender cream-and-chocolate vase from among the packing material. Tears came to her eyes and she hugged Jane again. "I'm overwhelmed. Thank you so much."

"You're welcome." Jane hesitated. "You could tell me more about the little theater. I might be able to give you some tips. Help out now and then."

"Oh, that's so exciting." Putting the vase back in its box, Leslie got to her feet. "I'm going to put this someplace safe. We'll talk later."

Leslie left. When Jane glanced around again, Cole was deep in conversation with

Joey. Disappointed, she poured herself more wine and moved down a few chairs to say hello to Valerie.

"I love how you fixed up the house," Mary Kate's grandmother said. "You're not going to let that awful woman tear it down, are you?"

"I suppose that's up to Cole."

Valerie tilted her head. "Oh? What does that mean?"

"I have to speak to him before I say anything."

"Then I'll go and let you two be alone." She squeezed Jane's hand. "You know, dear, you're part of the family, too. Whatever happens."

"Thank you, Valerie." Jane smiled, blinking.

"It's almost time for the cake," Valerie added. "I'm going to see if I can find some candles."

Valerie rose and called Joey to help her, leaving only one empty chair between Jane and Cole. It was dusk and the cockatoos were coming home to roost, their huge white wings flapping against the dark blue sky. Jane and Cole watched the birds settle into the silvery limbs of the old gum tree. Then they turned to each other. The atmosphere between them grew thick. The calls of the children and the laughter of the adults seemed to fade away. Yet neither seemed able to make the next move.

Jane counted the chairs on either side and slid over. "We meet in the middle."

"Sounds promising." Cole nodded at the envelope. "Did you sign it?"

She shook her head. "I can't let Mia tear down your great-grandfather's house."

Cole let out a sigh of relief. "Thank God. Joey's prepared to buy into the agency. I'll be able to purchase the farm after all."

"Good," Jane said. "And before you try to bargain me down, I want you to know that for you I'm cutting my price in half. I won't take a penny more."

Cole looked wary. "If you want me to sign something about Mary Kate—"

Jane stopped him with an upraised hand. "No. I was wrong. She's your daughter. I won't ever take her away from you again."

"Then there's only one thing that would make my happiness complete," he began.

"I know." She spoke quickly so she wouldn't lose her nerve. "Mary Kate wants so much to live here with you and Stephanie. I...I've been selfish, keeping her from you. I've been scared, too, that something will happen if I'm not there for her. It's not rational, I know. I...I have a suggestion."

"What is it?" Cole asked.

"We ask Mary Kate where she wants to live. If it's primarily with you and Stephanie, then so be it. It'll be hard for me to get used to, but I'll buy a house in Red Hill so I can be close. The arrangement seems to work for you and Leslie."

"Well, it won't work for us," Cole said with feeling. "Not for one second."

Jane bit her lip, scanning his face. "What do you want?"

"I told you what I want. You and me together. The four of us living as a family."

"But...you'd have Mary Kate. I don't understand."

Cole took her hand and twined his fingers with hers. "*You* were my dream before I ever thought about buying back Cockatoo Ridge or owning my own vineyard. Before I ever thought about having children. I loved you so much. I never stopped. Don't get me wrong, Stephanie and Mary Kate mean the world to me, but my happiness won't be complete without you."

Tears sprang to Jane's eyes. Her throat went thick and she struggled to breathe, to speak. "Oh, Cole. I thought you just wanted Mary Kate."

He gathered her in his arms. "I'm sorry I ever said those awful words, telling you I didn't love you. I was young and confused, shoehorned into a life I never asked for. I did what I had to, for my family. I'm so sorry that I hurt you."

"I'm sorry that I didn't spend more time here, that you lost those years with Mary Kate." She lifted her face and kissed him. "We have a lot of catching up to do."

Just then Valerie and Leslie came out of the house bearing a huge chocolate cake blazing with candles. "'Happy birthday to you, happy birthday to you…'"

Cole slid his arm around Jane's waist and whispered in her ear, "I hear chocolate is an aphrodisiac."

She chuckled against his neck. "I guess we'll find out, won't we?"

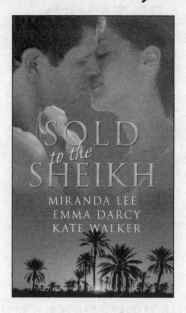

2 Books
and a surprise gift!

We would like to take this opportunity to thank you for reading this Mills & Boon® book by offering you the chance to take TWO more specially selected titles from the Superromance series absolutely FREE! We're also making this offer to introduce you to the benefits of the Mills & Boon® Book Club™—

- ★ FREE home delivery
- ★ FREE gifts and competitions
- ★ FREE monthly Newsletter
- ★ Exclusive Mills & Boon Book Club offers
- ★ Books available before they're in the shops

Accepting these FREE books and gift places you under no obligation to buy, you may cancel at any time, even after receiving your free shipment. Simply complete your details below and return the entire page to the address below. You don't even need a stamp!

YES! Please send me 2 free Superromance books and a surprise gift. I understand that unless you hear from me, I will receive 4 superb new titles every month for just £3.69 each, postage and packing free. I am under no obligation to purchase any books and may cancel my subscription at any time. The free books and gift will be mine to keep in any case.

U9ZEF

Ms/Mrs/Miss/Mr .... Initials ....
BLOCK CAPITALS PLEASE

Surname ....

Address ....

....

.... Postcode ....

Send this whole page to:
UK: FREEPOST CN81, Croydon, CR9 3WZ

Offer valid in UK only and is not available to current Mills & Boon Book Club subscribers to this series. Overseas and Eire please write for details. We reserve the right to refuse an application and applicants must be aged 18 years or over. Only one application per household. Terms and prices subject to change without notice. Offer expires 31st August 2009. As a result of this application, you may receive offers from Harlequin Mills & Boon and other carefully selected companies. If you would prefer not to share in this opportunity please write to The Data Manager, PO Box 676, Richmond, TW9 1WU.

Mills & Boon® is a registered trademark owned by Harlequin Mills & Boon Limited.
The Mills & Boon® Book Club™ is being used as a trademark.